KELLAN

ANNA BLAKELY

KELLAN

Charlie Team Series 1

Anna Blakely

Kellan

Charlie Team Book 1

First Edition
Copyright © 2021 Anna Blakely
All rights reserved.
All cover art and logo Copyright © 2021
Proofreading by Christine Hall, Kim Ruiz, Angie Springs
Copy Editing by Tracy Roelle

All rights reserved. No part of this book may be reproduced in any form or by any electronic or mechanical means, including information storage and retrieval systems—except in the case of brief quotations embodied in critical articles or reviews—without permission in writing from the author.

This book is a work of fiction. The names, characters, and places portrayed in this book are entirely products of the author's imagination or used fictitiously. Any resemblance to actual events, locales, or persons, living or dead, is entirely coincidental and not intended by the author.

The unauthorized reproduction or distribution of this copyrighted work is illegal. Criminal copyright infringement, including infringement without monetary gain, is investigated by the FBI and is punishable by up to five years in federal prison and a fine of $250,000.00.

If you find any eBooks being sold or shared illegally, please contact the author at anna@annablakely.com.

❋ Created with Vellum

ABOUT THE BOOK

She thought she was free, but her past refuses to let her go.

Mia Devereaux escaped from hell, and she has the scars to prove it. Two years later, she's still looking over her shoulder, afraid to let her guard down or open her heart to the possibility of more. Then she meets Kellan McBride.

Former Marine Kellan McBride is a man who knows danger. As an operative for RISC's new Charlie Team, he continues to protect the innocent by giving his job—and his teammates—his all. But there's something about Mia that sets his heart on fire and tilts his carefully planned world on its axis. He knows he should stay away from the quiet blonde with eyes that hold too many secrets, but their connection is too strong to ignore.

When Mia's past resurfaces and danger finds her once more, Kellan is determined to protect the woman he's falling in love with. Vowing to hunt down the darkness threatening her, he'll keep Mia safe and end her terror once and for all. Because if he can't, he may lose the woman who's captured his heart and soul—forever.

This book is for anyone who's ever picked up a R.I.S.C. book and loved it enough to want to read more. It is because of you that this new series exists.

AUTHOR'S NOTE

Well, here we are. Another R.I.S.C. Team in the making! I have to say, when I was finishing up the last book of the original series, I hadn't planned to continue with another R.I.S.C. team. But you spoke and I listened, and thus Kellan and the other members of Charlie Team were born.

The first couple to kickstart this new spinoff series is Kellan and Mia. After an accidental meeting, these two form a connection neither fully understands. But it's that connection that brings them together for the fight—and love—of their lives.

Thank you all so much for asking for this new team. I can't tell you how happy I am that you did, and I hope I've done you and these characters justice.

Happy Reading!
Anna

PROLOGUE

Two years ago...

Mia Devereaux sat alone in the silence. The shadows of the dark room blended to create a welcoming blanket that hid the beautiful home's frightening truth.

It happened so quickly this time. There'd been no warning. No feeling or a reflexive instinct that usually presented itself by way of a slow work-up to her husband's violent outburst.

Over the past three years, Mia had learned to recognize the signs. Little by little, he'd start to lose the tight grip on his control until eventually, he'd explode with an unhinged rage.

Elliot would yell and scream. This would escalate into hitting or kicking. Sometimes both. Then he'd disappear for hours on end, leaving her alone in the darkness.

Later, once the dust had settled and he felt she'd enough time to think about what it was she'd done to cause it all, her husband would come back home. Hands that had caused so much pain would hold flowers or an elaborate piece of jewelry.

These meaningless gifts were always accompanied by an empty apology and promises that would make Mia's stomach churn. But not this time. No, tonight was different.

Tonight had changed everything.

Mia had been in the kitchen preparing dinner when Elliot had gotten home late from work. She'd asked what had kept him out so late—an innocent inquiry meant only as a cordial conversation starter.

Instead, Elliot had immediately grown defensive. Within seconds, he was spewing profanities and throwing things around.

Dishes broke against the wall. The vase filled with freshly cut flowers she'd carefully arranged earlier that day had shattered on the room's Spanish tile floor.

Pretty soon, he'd started throwing *her* around, too.

Into a wall. Down onto the floor. After a few kicks with his steel-toed boots, Elliot had used her hair to yank her to her bare feet and push her through the house and out their front door. Then he shoved her—hard—and she'd fallen down the concrete stairs leading to their secluded home's entrance.

That last part was the reason for the cast.

But the thing that made Elliot's most recent burst of abusive rage so different was what happened *after*.

Mia had been lying there on that final step, sobbing from the pain in her arm and her shattered heart. And Elliot, well…he'd pulled his gun from his holster and shoved it against the back of her skull.

Hours had passed since that life-altering moment, but she could still feel the cold, hard metal digging against her scalp. Though her pulse had since returned to its normal pace, her veins still carried the utter terror that had raced through them as she'd laid there waiting for him to pull the trigger.

It was the farthest Elliot had ever pushed things between them, and in that moment, Mia had been certain she was going to die. With no way to fight back, she'd done nothing but squeeze her eyes shut and wait for the end to come.

Mia was shocked when it didn't, but what surprised her even more was the sense of disappointment she'd felt as a result.

My God, I'd actually wanted him to do it.

Hurt and ashamed, Mia's tears had mixed with the slow trickle of chilling rain as she realized she'd been praying for him to pull that trigger. In her wounded mind, she'd begged him to end his reign of terror and control over her.

To set her free.

But he hadn't. Instead, Elliot had lowered the gun, helped her to her feet, and guided her back inside what she'd long ago coined the House of Horrors.

Of course, there'd been no visit to the hospital or calls to the police. There never was.

Hospitals meant medical records and questions she didn't dare answer. And the police, well… Mia learned a long time ago the deputies of North Carolina's Warsaw County were not on her side.

Only his.

Always his.

Instead, her husband had made a phone call and another man had come. One who'd been there before.

Bringing the glass of wine to her lips, Mia glanced down at the blue cast keeping her damaged radius immobile. Another round of tears threatened to spill from her red and swollen eyes, but she blinked them back, refusing to let them fall.

Tears were for sadness and regret. While she felt both of those things—and so much more—Mia's regret stemmed from not having found the strength to do this sooner, rather than waiting until things escalated to the point that they had tonight.

She'd always believed everything happened for a reason, but in those long, terrifying moments when she was *sure* Elliot was going to kill her, Mia couldn't see past her fear to understand what it all meant.

But now, sitting in the dark and wondering how she could let her life spiral out of control the way she had, everything had finally become crystal clear.

Every ounce of pain she'd experienced over the past two years—both physical and mental—had led her to this very moment. As much as she hated to admit it, tonight had been the necessary step to *finally* bring her to the place where she could accept what needed to be done.

Facing certain death at the hands of a man she'd once cherished was the final push her fractured soul needed to salvage what was left of her life. To recognize what she truly wanted...and what she deserved.

No more tears. No more living in fear. No more pain.

No more Elliot.

After another sip of the sweet liquid courage, Mia set the glass down onto the end table next to her and picked up the burner phone she'd kept hidden in a pot in the back of one of the kitchen cabinets. It had been given to her months ago by the most unlikely of sources, along with the promise to help her escape.

At the time, Mia had been too afraid to make the call.

But after what happened earlier this evening, the fear of staying overshadowed everything else.

Powering up the phone, she hesitated a fraction of a second before tapping on the one and only number saved in the device. Ringing filled the phone's speaker, the rolling sound making her heart pound against her ribs.

Nerves forced the air to leave her lungs at a faster pace as she waited, praying the person she was calling would pick up. Three rings later, he did.

"Mia?" The familiar male voice was laced with a hushed concern. "What happened? Are you okay?"

"No." Mia shook her head, angrily swiping at a tear that defied her will to contain it. She pushed past the pain in her arm and swallowed against the rising panic in her gut as she said, "But I will be, if you're still willing to help me."

Seconds of silence passed, and for a moment, she thought he'd changed his mind. Panic and despair left her breathless, but then she heard, "Of course, I'll help you. I told you before…whenever you're ready."

Was she ready?

She'd been so sure of herself a minute ago. But now that she was forced to say the words out loud, the same sliver of doubt that had stopped her from making the call before now reared its ugly head.

Don't listen to it, Mia. You have to do this. If you don't, there may not be another chance.

Her inner voice was right. Elliot hadn't pulled the trigger tonight, but what about next time? Would he stop?

The sickening knot in her stomach held the answer.

If she didn't leave tonight…*right now*…the man she'd once vowed to spend the rest of her life with would eventually kill her. Because it was no longer a matter of if, but when.

"I'm ready." Mia lifted her chin, her voice already sounding a bit stronger. "Just tell me what I need to do."

"Do you remember the place we talked about before? The old silos on the edge of town?"

"Yes."

"Meet me there."

"When?" She held her breath waiting for the answer.

Please say now. If we wait until later, Elliot might come back, and then—

"Now."

Nearly crying with relief, Mia's chin quivered as she blew out a dizzying breath. "I have a bag ready to go."

The large duffle on the floor near her feet was filled with five outfits, two pairs of shoes, a few toiletries, and the cash she'd managed to pigeon-hole away over the last several months without detection.

"Grab it and get the hell out of there. And Mia?"

"Yes?"

"Don't forget to leave your other phone there. If you take it, he'll be able to track you."

She'd already thought of that but hearing him say the words out loud made the whole scenario impossibly real.

"O-okay." Damn it, her voice was shaking again.

"Good girl. Now hang up and get out of there. I'll see you in just a few minutes. Oh, and Mia?"

"Yeah?"

"You walk out that door, don't ever look back."

Her head bobbed with a jerky nod. "I won't."

Mia stood from the couch. Sliding the burner phone into her pocket, she grabbed her bag and car keys, and left the wine on the end table.

Taking a step forward, she stopped mid-stride. Glancing

down at the half-empty glass, she did something she hadn't felt like doing in years.

Mia smiled.

In a move fueled solely by spite, she used her casted arm to knock the glass to the floor. Its deep crimson contents soaking into the pristine white carpet below.

Tried to tell you white would stain. Guess you should've listened to me.

He should've done a lot of things differently. So had she.

"Don't look back," Mia whispered to herself as she made her way to the home's elaborate front door.

And she didn't.

Disarming the alarm code so Elliot wouldn't be alerted, she kept her gaze forward, focusing on what lay ahead rather than what she was leaving behind.

Five minutes later, she was pulling up to the abandoned silos she and her friends had played hide-and-seek around when they were kids.

Back when her dreams still seemed attainable, and all she wanted out of life was to grow up, marry a man who loved her as much as she loved him, and raise a family.

Now the only dream she had was to survive.

Headlights flashed, illuminating the interior of her car. For a split second, Mia feared Elliot had somehow discovered her plan, but as the man got out of a car she didn't recognize and stepped into those lights, she saw him for who he really was.

Shane.

Grabbing her bag from the passenger seat, Mia got out of her car and walked to her husband's twin brother.

Brown eyes identical to Elliot's fell to her casted arm, filling with sympathy that made her heart sick.

"Oh, Mia." Shane stared back at her, a puff of white

escaping into the frigid air with his words. "I'm so fucking sorry."

Tall, dark, and exquisitely handsome, the man was an exact match to his brother...right down to his DNA. But there were two ways she always knew the difference between them.

Shane's genuinely kind, fun-loving personality was one. The scar on the left side of his forehead was the other.

"You're the only one in your family who's ever offered to help me." She gave her brother-in-law a sad smile. "You have nothing to be sorry for."

His brother and parents, however, could all go straight to hell.

"God, Mia. I don't even know what to say." Shane shook his head.

Mia shifted the bag's strap on her shoulder. "Nothing to say, Shane. I put myself into this position."

And now, after all this time, she was finally getting out.

"If I thought there was any other way—"

"There isn't." She stared up at him. "You and I both know what he's capable of. What the people of this town will continue to ignore. You said it yourself. The only way I'll ever truly be safe is if I disappear."

Those were the words Shane had whispered to her at the last big Devereaux family function. He'd caught a glimpse of the bruise she'd been trying to hide and had gotten worried for her. Pulling her aside, Shane had done his damnedest to convince her to leave that very night.

If only I'd listened to him then.

But she hadn't and playing the what-if game would get her nowhere.

"If he finds out you helped..." Mia didn't want to think about what Elliot would do.

"He won't," Shane spoke with confidence she wished she felt. "And before you ask, because I know you will, my car is parked within walking distance from here. As soon as you leave, I'll head back that way and drive into town for a drink. People will see me there and not think twice about my involvement in any of this. And as far as anyone will ever know, I was never here. The cops will find your car abandoned and assume you either ran off or were abducted." Reaching into his coat's interior chest pocket, he pulled out a small manila envelope and handed it to her. "Everything you need is in there."

Needing to be sure, Mia slid the contents out of the envelope and into her free hand. Sure enough, he was right.

Where he'd gotten it, she had no idea. But Shane had somehow managed to provide her with a new driver license, passport, and the title to a car matching the description of the one he'd driven here.

"Virginia?" She glanced up at him from the shiny new I.D.

A drivers license with her picture but the name Mia *Carpenter* instead of Mia Devereaux.

He used my great-grandmother's maiden name.

"There's a furnished apartment waiting for you in Richmond. Security deposit and the first six months have already been paid for. After that, it'll be up to you, but I know you'll find a job in no time."

Hopefully, he was right. She had a bachelor's degree, and before she and Elliot were married, she'd worked as a free-lance graphic designer. But first things, first.

"Shane, I—"

"Deserve to be happy." Gravel crunched beneath his boots as he stepped closer. "So go, Mia. Be happy."

Warm tears pricked the corners of her eyes. "Why couldn't I have fallen for you instead of Elliot?"

A playful smirk lifted Shane's thin lips. "I've asked myself that every day for the past three years."

Mia chuckled because she knew he was only teasing.

She and Shane had been good friends, but there had never been so much as a hint of attraction for either one of them. Which was strange, given that he looked exactly like the man she *had* fallen for.

A man who'd done a damn good job at hiding who he really was.

"Go on, now." He pulled her in for a brief but tight hug. Kissing the top of her head in a brotherly way, Shane guided her toward the new-to-her car. "Go find the life you've always wanted and forget about this fucking town and all its bullshit secrets."

Easier said than done, but she was damn sure going to try. "I won't forget you, Shane. Not ever."

"Same goes for me." He cupped one side of her face in that caring way he always had. "I love ya, Sis. Take care of yourself, yeah?"

"I will."

After another quick hug, Mia tossed her bag into the back seat and got behind the wheel. With one final glance at the only person willing to risk themselves to help her, she pulled out of the gravel lot and left that town—and her husband—behind.

1

Present day...

"Go! Go! Go!"

Following his leader's command, Kellan McBride ran alongside his new team, their boots thumping across dry land as they made their way to the nearest available cover. The rat-a-tat-tat of the firefight they were currently engaged in filled the humid, afternoon air.

Hunched down behind two of the tangos' vehicles, Kellan and the others remained low while working together to eliminate the enemy. Each fallen target bringing them that much closer to the package they'd been sent here to find.

"Reloading!" Kellan shouted as he leaned his back against one of the dust-covered cars.

Knowing his team had his six, he released the empty mag from his M4 carbine rifle, grabbed a backup from his vest, and slammed it into place. Pushing the bolt release,

Kellan injected a live round into the chamber before repositioning the weapon and taking aim.

Several shots were exchanged between his team and their targets. Countless rounds of hot metal pinged off the cars protecting them. Glass shattered as the tangos holding an American doctor hostage continued with their efforts to kill every member of RISC's new Charlie Team.

The elite black ops security firm Kellan and the others worked for consisted of three, all-former military teams, and each one was well-known amongst the country's private security sector.

The company started a few years ago with Alpha Team, which was still active and worked out of their headquarters in Dallas. Bravo Team was also stationed out of Texas, but when Jake McQueen—owner of RISC and Alpha Team's former leader—saw the need to expand, he decided to put together two new teams: Charlie and Delta.

Charlie Team was based out of Richmond, Virginia, and the Delta office was in Chicago. With the evils of this world growing exponentially by the day, so did the need for more teams like theirs.

"Intel said there were only six of these bastards." Asher Cross ducked quickly to avoid being hit.

The former Army Ranger let out a curse when a bullet narrowly missed striking his head. Unfazed by the close call, the youngest member of the team wasted no time balancing the barrel of his weapon on the top of the beat-up car's hood and taking out the tango who'd nearly killed him.

"Not the first time the higher-ups have gotten it wrong." The rumbled comment came from Greyson Frost, or Iceman, as his former SEAL Team used to call him. "Sure as hell won't be the last."

Tall and built like a brick shithouse, Kellan didn't know

how the guy fit his long hair under his combat helmet, but somehow the frogman managed to make it work.

"That intel doesn't mean shit at this point, boys!" Trace Winters, their team leader, hollered out over the barrage of gunfire. Taking out another tango, he reminded them all, "We just need to focus on clearing out the trash and getting Dr. Blake back home!"

"Copy that, Boss!" Kellan pulled his trigger again.

A loud grunt was followed by several wayward shots. Kellan's target reflexively squeezed his trigger as he fell to the ground with an ominous thud.

For the next several minutes, both groups of men returned fire until eventually, only one group was left standing.

Score one for the good guys.

"All right, boys," Rhys Maddox—Charlie Team's medic and all-around badass—drawled. "Time to find the girl and get the hell out of here."

With mumbled agreements, the five-man team booted past several lifeless bodies as they made their way to the previously guarded building.

Positioning themselves on either side of the front entrance, Greyson stuck the edge of a breach strip at the top right corner of the door. Rolling it along the wood hinge-side, he pressed the strip against the wood to ensure it remained in place long enough to do its job.

Kellan and the others kept their weapons up and their heads on a swivel, their trained eyes on constant lookout for any new threat that may come their way.

"We're a go," Greyson informed them all.

Without having to be told, the team moved a safe distance away, along the building's length. Greyson initiated the charge, the door exploding with a loud flash of fire. They didn't wait for the smoke to clear before moving in.

As always, Trace was first in line. Their team leader pushed the fallen door out of the way to make room for the rest of them, and without hesitations, Kellan, Asher, Greyson, and Rhys followed the former Delta Force operator into the unknown.

Two tangos were waiting to greet them, yelling something in Arabic while raising their weapons in Kellan and Trace's direction.

They didn't give the assholes the chance to fire.

Pulling his trigger, Kellan discharged his gun simultaneously with his leader's. The combined shots creating a deafening *boom* throughout the small space.

Moving as one, they continued making their way through the building. Each tango they crossed trying—and failing—to take Charlie Team out in the process. Instead, Kellan and the others sent them each straight to Hell.

Once the initial assault was over, they continued down a long hallway to the final two rooms at the back of the building. Muffled voices reached Kellan's ears, so he tapped on Trace's shoulder and pointed to one of the doors.

With a nod, Trace raised a fist in the air, stopping just before the indicated room. Kellan and the others followed suit. Halting their movements, they waited for the signal to enter.

Trace silently motioned for Rhys and Greyson to go around them to the next room over. They'd need to breach both rooms at the same time to prevent putting themselves —or the hostage—at risk of an attack from behind.

Waiting for the two men to get into position, Trace gave the team a single nod. A second later, both doors were kicked in, and the final bullets from Charlie Team's latest mission were set free.

Like before, Kellan and Trace pulled their triggers the instant their targets came into view. Two local insurgents who'd had the unfortunate task of guarding their American hostage were now dead, their lives wasted for a meaningless and violent cause.

"All clear!" Rhys informed them from the hallway.

"Good." Turning back around, Trace gave the other man an approving nod. "You and Frost double-check the perimeter. I know we cleared it before, but this place is secluded as fuck. I want to make sure we didn't miss anyone before we take the package out in the open."

"Copy that." Rhys gave the man in charge a sloppy salute, and he and Greyson vanished back down the hall toward the building's entrance.

While that conversation was taking place, Asher had already gone to the woman still tied to a chair in the far corner of the room. Kellan didn't miss the gentle way with which his teammate approached her.

"Dr. Blake, my name is Asher Cross." Asher removed his tactical goggles and kept his tone soft and non-threatening. "We're Americans, and we're here to take you home."

Gagged with a dirty rag, the woman—who looked even younger in person than in the picture they'd been provided—hung her head in relief and cried.

"I'm going to untie you now." Asher gave her a friendly smile as he told her exactly what he was going to do before he did it.

It was a tactic they'd all learned in their early military careers. Hostages—both men and women—were unpredictable in how they reacted to being rescued.

Some cried. Others remained silent for the entirety of

the trip home. Some even lashed out at them, their tortured minds unable to accept the reality that they were the good guys, and that their terrifying experience was finally over.

From the amount of time they'd spent being held against their will to the treatment they'd received by their captors, the men and women Kellan and the others had helped rescue in the past taught them all the importance of proceeding with caution.

He, Trace, and Greyson waited patiently while Asher pulled the rough ropes holding Dr. Blake's wrists to the chair's wooden arms free. First one, and then the other, the former Ranger winced as he helped the shaken woman to her feet.

Following his teammate's gaze, Kellan found the source of Asher's empathetic pain. Angry red marks and dried blood marred the delicate skin covering Dr. Blake's wrists. Proof she'd fought hard to get loose.

Fucking bastards.

Kellan slid his focus to the two dead men lying in pools of their own blood. He wanted to kill them again for ever having laid a hand on the poor woman. A woman who, from what they'd been told during their initial briefing, had come to Abu Dhabi as part of the Doctors Without Borders program.

Contrary to what many believed, terrorist attacks in this particular city were a rare occurrence. Of course, rare didn't mean never, and Dr. Blake apparently had the unfortunate luck to be in the wrong place at the wrong time.

But Kellan and his team had found her in time, and the men responsible for her capture had been dealt a swift and heavy hand.

They were God's problem now. Or, more accurately, the Devil's.

"Thank you." Dr. Blake's feminine voice sounded dry and rough as she removed the gag from her mouth.

Dirt and dried blood matted her long, dark hair, and bruises marred her skin. Fresh blood seeped from a split in her lip, evidence of the violence she'd been subjected to.

Dropping it to the concrete floor below, she let her watery blue gaze fall on each man in the room. "I thought..." She cleared her throat and jutted her chin. "I thought they were going to kill me. They *would* have killed me if you hadn't shown up when you did. So, while it doesn't even come close to being enough...thank you."

"Just doing our job, Dr. Blake," Asher offered.

She gave him a hint of a smile and said, "It's Sydnee."

Asher smiled back at her, and if Kellan wasn't mistaken, there was a glimmer of admiration—and something else he couldn't quite name—in the young man's brown eyes.

Interesting.

"Perimeter's clear, Boss." Rhys appeared in the open doorway while Greyson stood off to the side.

"What do you say, Sydnee?" Trace addressed the woman they'd been hired to rescue. "You ready to go home?"

A fresh onslaught of tears glistened in her eyes as she gave the man in charge a nod. "Yes, please."

Kellan watched as Asher hovered protectively near the pretty brunette doctor. The man was clearly smitten, and Kellan didn't have the heart to warn him away.

One, Dr. Sydnee Blake was way out of Asher's league. And two, guys like them...they simply weren't built for relationships.

Trace would probably disagree with you on that, considering he's getting married and all.

The voice in his head had a point. Winters wasn't just

engaged; he was marrying Emma Cooper, Charlie Team's adorable and quirky office manager.

According to Trace, the two had met right before some asshole tried to ruin the entire RISC organization by blowing up their main office in Dallas... With Trace, Emma, and the entire Alpha Team inside.

Luckily, they all made it out alive. Even luckier, or so Trace tells it, the crazy experience had led their leader to the woman of his dreams.

We'll see how long it lasts.

Kellan knew the thought was pessimistic as hell, but that didn't mean he was wrong. He'd learned a long time ago that love and all the bullshit that comes with it simply wasn't worth it.

"I don't know about the rest of you"—Greyson blew out a breath as they exited the building—"but I could sure use a beer right about now."

Slapping the big guy on one of his massive shoulders, Kellan walked beside him as they made their way to their borrowed van. "I think that's the best idea I've heard this whole trip, brother."

Twenty-four hours later, Kellan was rested, showered, and walking out of his apartment in Richmond to go meet up with the guys for that beer.

After leaving Abu Dhabi, the team had first flown Dr. Blake—*Sydnee*—to Homeland Security's private medical facility in Dallas so she could be cleaned up and checked over by their doctors before giving her full statement and account of her capture. After that, she'd been escorted to her home in D.C.

From experience, Kellan knew the woman was asked to

share every single detail she could remember from the time she'd been forced to spend with the insurgents to when he and his team had shown up.

While Sydnee was being cared for by the hospital's staff, Kellan and the others had each given Jason Ryker—RISC's official Homeland handler and the man who'd sent them on the mission to start with—a brief rundown of what had taken place.

After, the five-man team had gotten onto one of RISC's three private jets for the two-and-a-half-hour flight home to Virginia.

This morning, Charlie Team had met at their office located in a non-descript high-rise in downtown Richmond to type up their official debriefing statements, discuss them, and make sure they didn't leave anything out before sending them on.

Despite their short time together—they'd only been an active team executing missions for a couple of months—the five men had already formed a tight bond. One Kellan was certain would only grow stronger as their time together spanned on.

Stopped at a red light a few blocks from the bar where he was meeting the guys, Kellan was so lost in his thoughts that he didn't notice the car approaching him too quickly from behind.

Not until he felt a sudden jolt from the impact.

As the other vehicle made contact, his body was flung forward in his seat, his right foot instinctively going to the break. Kellan's seatbelt did its job, locking into place and keeping him from slamming into his steering wheel.

Thankfully whoever had just rear-ended him hadn't been going fast enough to push him into oncoming traffic.

"Great." Kellan sighed as he slid his gearshift to park.

Releasing the buckle securing him to his seat, he opened his door and got out, praying the guy wasn't going to be a giant prick about the whole thing. But when the driver got out to join him on the quiet side street, Kellan realized it wasn't a guy at all.

It was a woman.

A petite woman with shoulder length, cornsilk hair and the biggest green eyes he'd ever seen. She was dressed in a pair of snug jeans that showcased her slight curves, and a cream-colored sweater that hid what he could tell were perfectly proportioned breasts.

She was staring back at him, her gaze filled with regret and fear as she rushed toward him. And she was…

Fucking beautiful.

"Are you okay?" she hurried to ask. "I-I'm so sorry. I thought I saw…" The woman looked over her shoulder then shook her head. "It doesn't matter. Are you okay?"

The quivering in her voice was laced with fear, and for some reason all Kellan wanted to do was make it disappear.

"I'm fine." he assured her. His eyes swept down the length of her tempting body. "Are *you* okay?"

She didn't seem to be hurt, but adrenaline could often mask pain while it was still pumping through a person's system. Something he and every man on his team knew first-hand.

"I-I'm fine." Her wary gaze remained on his. "I'm so sorry."

With another assessing once-over, Kellan concluded that she was, in fact, okay. Her car, on the other hand…

He squatted down to check out the large dent in the Accord's front fender and hood. "Doesn't look too bad." Tilting his head to the side, he listened for a beat at the engine's steady purr. "Sounds like it's still running okay."

"Oh, thank God." Relief seemed to flood her entire system. "Of course, the important thing is that you're not hurt. Wait here!"

As the gorgeous stranger began looking inside her car for something, Kellan stood straight and looked at the back of his. There were a few new scratches on his bumper, but other than that, it appeared to be fine.

Thank you, steel bumpers!

"Here."

Kellan lifted his head to find her staring back at him with her checkbook and pen in hand. Brows furrowed, he asked, "What are you doing?"

"Covering the damage to your bumper. I can see the scratches I caused, so just tell me how much you think it'll cost to repair it, and then we can both be on our way."

The offer didn't come off as snobby or uncaring. No, there was another reason this little five-feet-nothing woman was trying to buy him off and leave the scene.

She glanced over her shoulder again, as if to check for cars that might be headed their way. Except he noticed her eyes weren't on the road...they were on the sidewalk to his right.

Kellan's mind began replaying the incident. When she'd first gotten out of her car, she'd mentioned seeing something. Or rather, *thinking* she'd seen something. But she'd never said what.

Add to that her nervous mannerisms and the skittish way she was acting and his gut said something more was at play than a little bumper-to-bumper action. After all, who gets in a wreck and immediately starts throwing money at the person they hit?

Someone who doesn't want to involve the cops.

With an unwavering gaze, Kellan studied her with an operative's eye.

The woman before him was clearly shaken, but that could simply mean that this was the first fender-bender she'd been in. Of course, it was quite possible he was reading too much into things. That *was* an occupational hazard for guys like him.

But his gut was telling him that wasn't the case.

The more he watched her, the more Kellan was certain there was something more at play than a simple case of nerves. And his curiosity refused to let it go.

"Are you sure *you're* okay?" He pulled his phone from his pocket. A test to see how she would react. "Maybe we should report this and let the cops—"

"No!" She made a move as if she were going to move closer to him but stopped. "I-I mean, there's really no need to involve the authorities, is there? You said yourself, it wasn't that bad. And I've offered to cover the damages, so if you'll just give me a number—"

"Five thousand dollars." Kellan schooled his expression as he waited for her reaction.

"O-oh." The woman blinked those big eyes and began to ramble. "Um...o-okay. That's a little more than I was thinking, but...sure. I can transfer some money from my savings as soon as I get home. But I don't know if it'll hit my checking account until morning, so if you don't mind waiting until tomorrow to cash this..."

She actually started writing the check. An act that was surprising all on its own. But what really struck Kellan as strange was how badly the checkbook trembled as she began penning the numbers. That and the way she glanced back at the sidewalk...*again*.

Then it hit him.

This woman wasn't shaken up from bumping into him. She was terrified of whatever—or whoever—she thought she saw that *caused* her to hit him.

She's running from something.

Of that, Kellan was almost certain. But what?

"Stop." His gruff order accompanied a step toward her and a hand reaching toward hers.

The woman started at the command, her entire body tensing as she took a step backward. Putting a safe distance between them, her eyes flew to his. "W-what is it?" she stammered nervously. "What's w-wrong?"

Way to go, asshole. You've scared her even more.

"Put the checkbook away." Kellan forced a gentle voice. "I was only kidding about the five grand. Bad joke. Sorry."

"Really?" Suspicion warred with relief in her unsettled gaze. "Because I can cover the cost of the—"

"Really." He put a hand up to wave her offer to pay him away. Motioning toward his Jeep, he told her, "This thing has had a lot worse done to it. Trust me."

Her shoulders fell with a soft sigh. "Thank you. That's really nice of you."

"Not a big deal."

"No, it is. And...I apologize again for hitting you. I should've been paying better attention to where I was going."

"It's okay," Kellan felt his lips curve slightly. "We can chalk it up to a lesson learned, yeah?"

"Definitely." She blushed, giving him a chagrined smile.

The move exposed a single dimple in her left cheek he found adorable.

"Okay, then." Kellan nodded. "Be careful driving to... wherever it is you were headed."

"Groceries." The blonde chuckled nervously. "I was just going to get a few groceries and then head back home."

"Well, wherever that is, drive safe."

"Thank you." She started for her car but stopped just before she got inside. Turning back toward him, she said, "I didn't even ask your name."

"It's Kellan."

"Kellan." Another smile almost reached her pretty eyes. "I like that. I'm Mia."

The name seemed to fit her. "Nice to meet you, Mia."

"You, too."

And with that, *Mia* got into her car, and he slid behind the wheel of his Jeep.

A COUPLE HOURS LATER, AS HE SAT WITH THE GUYS AT Thirsty's—the bar they'd recently started going to after completing each job—Kellan was still thinking about the pretty blonde with the wary eyes.

Part of him regretted not taking her money. Not because he would've actually *cashed* the check, but because then he'd have her full name and address. Although...

"Hey, Grey." He turned to Greyson who was sitting in the chair to his right. "You got your tablet out in your truck?"

"Don't I always?" The man's deep voice rumbled over the music as he gathered his hair in one of his big fists to slide it off his shoulders.

"I'm guessing if McBride knew the answer to that, he wouldn't have asked," Asher smarted off.

Ignoring the youngest member of their team, Greyson took a long draw of his fresh beer and swallowed before turning his golden eyes to Kellan's. "Yes, I have my tablet." He sat his tall glass down. "What do you need?"

"If I give you a plate, can you run it for a name and address?"

One of Greyson's dark brows arched incredulously. "Did you seriously just ask me that?"

Right. Of *course*, the former SEAL could find out that shit. The tall bastard wasn't just a master at demolitions. He was also the team's technical analyst. And though he may not look the part, when it came to digging up intel, Greyson Frost was a fucking genius.

Grabbing a clean napkin, Kellan used the pen their server had left behind earlier to scribble the numbers and letters he'd memorized from Mia's license plate.

"First name's Mia. At least, that's what she told me."

Greyson took the napkin from him. "You don't believe her?"

"I don't know, yet." Kellan had filled them in on the fender bender when he'd first arrived at the bar. "But she sure wigged the hell out when I mentioned reporting it to the cops. It didn't matter to me. Her car took the brunt of the hit." He shrugged. "Only reason I mentioned it was to see how she'd react."

"And?"

"She offered to write me a check right there in the street to cover the scratches on my bumper."

"You take the money?" Asher asked.

"Hell, no, I didn't take it." Kellan swallowed another sip of his beer. "She asked how much, so I threw out a number."

"How much?"

"Five grand."

Asher let out a low whistle. "Damn. She ding you up that bad?"

"No. Like I said, it was just a few scratches."

Rhys frowned. "And she still agreed to pay the five thousand?"

"Yep." He motioned for their server to bring the table another round. "I mean, who does that?"

"Someone who doesn't want a ticket," Greyson proposed.

"Or she didn't want the cops running her name through the system." Rhys leaned his elbows on the table, the suspicion in his dark eyes matching Kellan's. "This woman say why she didn't want to report the accident?"

Kellan shook his head. "I didn't ask."

"Why the hell not?" the dark-haired man demanded.

"I don't know." Kellan ran a hand over his jaw. "She looked...scared."

More like fucking terrified.

Rhys scoffed. "Of course, she was scared. Woman's probably got a warrant issued for her ass. Hell, for all you know, she could be a psycho killer."

Kellan pictured the tiny blonde again. He envisioned staring into those green eyes of hers. Remembered the fear he'd found there.

Yeah, something was definitely going on with Mia—if that was even her real name. He just wished like hell he knew what it was.

Bet your ass, I'm going to find out.

"I'll run the plate as soon as we head out," Greyson announced. But then the big guy's lips curved into a sly smile. Rubbing his fingers along his trimmed beard, he added, "You know, if you wanted to learn more about this woman, you could've just asked her out."

"Nah, it's not like that."

The other man's amber eyes studied him closely. "You sure?"

"Yes, asshole. I'm sure." Kellan took a sip from his beer.

Sure, he wanted to know more about her, because if his gut was right—which it usually was—the beautiful woman with the haunted eyes was in trouble.

He didn't know what kind, but he damn sure intended to find out.

2

Lightning flashed across the afternoon sky as the predicted rainstorm approached the city of Richmond. Forcing herself to step away from the window, Mia made sure the blinds were closed, and the curtains were pulled tight. She hugged herself as she paced through the shadows filling her modest living room.

It was him. I know it was him.

Or maybe it wasn't. Maybe the man she'd seen yesterday—the one Mia could've sworn was Elliot—had been someone else entirely. Or maybe there hadn't been a man at all, and maybe…

She stopped in the middle of the room and blew out a breath. Hell, maybe she'd finally lost her damned mind.

Closing her eyes, Mia refilled her lungs before deflating them again. Slowly, this time.

In her mind's eye, she replayed the previous day's scene for the umpteenth time, going through it with as much detail as she could remember.

She'd been driving down the street, going through the mental list of things she needed from the store when she'd spotted him. It had been a quick, split-second moment in time, but Mia was *certain* Elliot had been the one walking down the sidewalk.

She could still feel the way her heart had leapt into her throat as she watched him stroll along as if he didn't have a care in the world. And when he caught sight of her oncoming car, he'd stopped and turned his head toward her. Those dark eyes, which held nothing but pain and misery, had locked onto hers as she'd driven past.

Even now, in the comfort and safety of her apartment, Mia's body trembled with fear. A fear only one man had ever created. A man she'd spent the last two years hiding from.

"No." She shook her head and dropped her arms to her sides. "He will not do this to me. Not again."

Never again.

It was bad enough she'd let a ghost from her past distract her to the point she'd caused an accident. Thank God no one was hurt, but if they had been...if she'd hit that man much harder, or a kid had been crossing the street...

She closed her eyes again, thanking her lucky stars that hadn't been the case. Instead, she'd struck the back of a man's jeep. A man who'd sent her heart racing for an entirely different reason.

Another set of eyes flashed before her. These weren't dark and evil like Elliot's. No, these were intelligent, sexy, steely gray eyes that saw much more than they should.

Kellan.

Mia liked that name. She liked it—and those eyes she could get lost in—a lot. And that was a dangerous thing.

Her stomach growled, reminding her of the fact that she'd never made it to the store as planned. After the incident with Kellan's Jeep, she'd been too shaken up to go anywhere but home.

The rumbling in her stomach grew louder, a nagging reminder that she needed sustenance. Since she never made it to the store yesterday, Mia decided to go now, before the storm set in.

Damn it.

Another bolt of lightning flashed behind her covered windows. This one was followed by a stretch of rolling thunder. A sign that she'd better hurry.

Double damn it.

Sliding into her slip-on canvas shoes, she grabbed her jacket, keys, and purse, and headed out the door. Locking it behind her—something she never, ever forgot to do—Mia made her way through the covered walkway to her car in the apartment complex's parking lot.

Just as it had several times this past week, the hair on the back of her neck stood on end. Her gut tightened, and she felt as if someone were watching her. But as she looked around, Mia saw nothing but streetlamps and empty cars.

No one's there, Mia. Get yourself together.

Determined to ignore the paranoia still running through her veins, she kept her eyes on the road ahead of her and pushed away the past. An hour later, the groceries were loaded, and Mia was headed back home when the skies opened, and the rain began to pour.

Flipping her windshield wipers on high, she squinted to see the lines on the two-lane highway she usually took as a shortcut back to her apartment. It saved time by allowing her to bypass the stretch of stoplights between the store and her complex.

It didn't hurt that it also kept her from driving past the scene of yesterday's bumpy greeting with the sexy Kellan.

He's not sexy. He's...a stranger. One you'll never see again.

The tiny voice was right. She needed to forget all about those smoky gray eyes and the way Kellan's t-shirt had stretched over what had to be a taut, sculpted chest.

Mia...

Gah! Seriously. What was she doing?

She had absolutely *no* business thinking about him—or any other man—like that. One, she was still technically married, and two... Mia sighed.

And two, she'd already proven her taste in men left something to be desired.

Shaking those thoughts away, she focused on the remainder of her drive. The rain was starting to let up some, but it was still coming down at a fairly steady pace.

Knowing a sharp curve was up ahead, Mia remembered what her father had taught her years before about breaking hard in the rain. Not wanting to hydroplane, she slid her right foot over to the brake pedal and pressed down gently.

Nothing happened.

Frowning, she put a little more pressure on the pedal with the ball of her foot. Again, her car didn't react.

What the...

Ignoring her father's timeless warning, she shoved the brake down as far as it would go. The resistance she should've felt was missing, the pedal touching the floorboard with ease.

Her brakes weren't working. At. All.

"Oh, shit."

With white-knuckled fists, Mia gripped the steering wheel tightly as she stared at the upcoming curve. Trees lined that section of the road, and it didn't take a genius to know that hitting them at her current speed of fifty-six miles per hour would make for a very bad day.

Emergency brake!

Praying she wasn't going to spin herself out of control, she kept her left hand on the wheel and used her right to reach toward her center console. Doing her best to remain calm, Mia grabbed the emergency brake and gave it a gentle pull.

Nothing.

Her stomach dropped. Fear racing through her veins, Mia pulled the brake with more force than before, but her efforts were all in vain.

Oh, God!

Headlights caught her rearview mirror as another vehicle approached her from behind. With no way of stopping her vehicle and the curve was getting closer by the second, Mia knew her only option was to try to stay on the road.

She put both hands back onto the wheel and held on for dear life.

The car swerved to the right as she turned with the curve. The back end jerked slightly, but when it straightened itself back out, Mia thought she was in the clear. Then it happened.

Feeling as though she was floating over a sheet of ice, the car began to hydroplane.

No!

Everything seemed to happen in slow motion.

The back of her car fish-tailed, sending Mia into a vicious spin. She screamed as the front turned to face the vehicle that had been behind her. Blinding lights filled the interior of her car a split second before she whipped back around the other way.

Her car continued to spin along the pavement's length. Her tires hit the road's graveled shoulder, causing Mia to slide down the steep embankment separating the road from the trees.

Though she hadn't been traveling at an excessive speed, the inability to slow down before the curve not only caused the initial hydroplane, but it also sent her car tumbling onto its side.

Pain exploded inside her head as she was thrown forcefully against the driver's side window. Over and over again, the car rolled across wet grass and fallen leaves, and all Mia could do was wait for it to stop.

When it did, her head was pounding and something warm and wet was running down the side of her face. She had the fleeting thought of searching for her phone and calling for help, but the rhythmic sound of the raindrops splattering against her cracked windshield combined with her wiper's steady motor was oddly soothing.

Letting her eyes fall shut—*just for a second*—Mia sat buckled in her crumpled car as the darkness began pulling her under. But then a loud banging on her window startled her.

How the damn thing didn't shatter in the wreck was a mystery. One she didn't have the energy or thought process to solve.

"Mia!" someone yelled for her.

Still stunned from the knock to her head, Mia blinked and turned toward the source. Standing in the pouring rain was a man.

"Hang on, I'm going to get you out!"

She blinked again, squinting against the throbbing pain and blurred vision. The man, whoever he was, had called her by her first name.

He knows me.

But Mia didn't know anyone in Richmond. Not really.

After moving here from North Carolina, she'd done everything she could to avoid people for fear someone would recognize her.

She'd bleached her hair and eyebrows blonde, dressed in plain, non-descript clothes. And other than the emails she and her clients exchanged, Mia didn't talk to anyone other than the delivery people bringing her food, the occasional polite greeting to a passing neighbor, and the checkout person at the gas station or grocery store.

For all intents and purposes, she was pretty much a hermit.

The man outside cursed loudly, the gruff bark momentarily yanking Mia from her rambling thoughts.

"Door's jammed," he yelled over the rain. "I'm going to try the passenger's side!"

Mia started to nod but winced when a giant wave of dizziness struck. Suddenly nauseated, it was all she could do to keep from throwing up.

It could be him. I need to get out of here.

Metal screeched and the car jostled as the passenger door was pulled free. With the headlights from his car behind him, the man looked like nothing more than a giant shadow with muscles, but when he ducked his head inside, she caught a glimpse of his handsome face.

Kellan.

Water dripped from his drenched hair and skin as his lips curved upward. "You remembered."

"What?"

"You said my name."

She frowned. "I did?"

Wiping the water from his face, Kellan lifted his gaze to the side of her head and frowned. "You've got a pretty good gash up there. Do you hurt anywhere else?"

"I-I don't think so."

She wiggled her fingers and toes, then did a quick mental rundown of the rest of her body. The airbags had deployed, and her chest felt a little tight from when the seatbelt had locked up, but other than that and her head, Mia was pretty sure she was okay.

"Good." Kellan spoke up again. "Just sit tight. The ambulance is on its way."

Mia's heart slammed against her ribs. "You called the police?"

His guarded stare met hers. "That a problem?"

Shit. Shit. Shit.

"I don't... I-I don't need an ambulance." She moaned. "I'm fine."

"Sweetheart, you just rolled your car about a billion times and your head is bleeding like a stuck pig. You're not fine."

"Y-you don't understand." She reached down to unbuckle her seatbelt.

He'll find me.

"Who?"

Mia tried pressing the buckle free again, but the dang thing was stuck.

Covering her hand, Kellan halted her frantic movements. "You said 'he'll find me'. Who are you talking about? Who will find you?"

Damn it. She really needed to start paying better attention to what she was saying versus what she was thinking.

"N-no one," she lied. "I just meant—"

Sirens blared in the distance, the piercing sound cutting through the easing storm.

Oh, God.

Overwhelming fear had Mia pressing the button once

more. Much to her relief, it disengaged, and she was able to yank the seatbelt free.

"I have to get out of here." She searched in vain for a way out of the car. "Please. You have to move. I can't be here when the police show up."

"Why not?" Kellan didn't budge. "What did you do?"

"Do?" She glared at him angrily. "The only thing I *did* was survive."

Kellan's stormy eyes searched for more as the sirens grew louder and then slowed to a whining stop. Though he looked like he wanted to say more, Kellan slid out of the car and into the rain, hollering up at the EMS crew.

"Down here!"

Two paramedics carefully made their way through the wet grass toward them. While they worked to place the extrication collar around Mia's neck, she noticed two police cars parking at the top of the hill near the ambulance.

Sirens off, their blue and red lights reflected off the glossy rain covering her car's damaged windshield. Their brightness was a source of anxiety and increased pain in her injured head.

Closing her eyes, Mia conceded to the fact that she had no choice but to allow the medics to pull her safely from the vehicle and place her onto a bright yellow backboard. Once she was secure, she floated as the two men carried her up the embankment and past Kellan, who was talking with two uniformed officers who'd arrived on scene.

Placing her onto a gurney, the paramedics slid her into the back of the ambulance as smoothly as possible. Warmth from the vehicle's heater soothed the goosebumps covering her chilled skin.

With one medic standing by the back bumper, the other

climbed up inside. The silver-haired man smiled down at her as he began dressing her head wound.

"What's your name?" he asked, moving to her inner right elbow to prep it for an I.V.

"Mia."

"Well, Mia, I'm Rob. Now, I just want you to try to relax. I'm going to take good care of you."

Try to relax.

Those were the same words she'd heard from a different medical professional on countless occasions. A doctor who'd sold his soul in exchange for Elliot turning a blind eye to his illegal ways.

Like him, this gentleman tried making small talk, explaining what he was doing and why. His kindness was appreciated, but Mia had enough experience with physical injuries, she was more than a little familiar with the routine.

"I'll follow you to the hospital."

Those words came from Kellan who was standing out of Mia's line of sight. She started to tell him it wasn't necessary, but the ambulance doors slammed shut before she had the chance.

With no other choice, she made the conscious choice to close her eyes and shut out the rest of the world. They'd either discover her real identity, or they wouldn't.

At this point, Mia wasn't sure it mattered anymore.

Because if that man she'd seen on the sidewalk yesterday really *was* Elliot, then it was only a matter of time before he made his move. And when that happened, not even God would be able to help her.

3

COLD AND DAMP, Kellan stood outside Mia's room waiting for the okay to go in and see her. With his back against the stark white wall and his legs crossed at his ankles, he stared at the closed door as he tried—and failed—to ignore the images flashing through his mind.

He could still see Mia's car flipping over itself down that fucking embankment. Kellan could still feel the rush of *fear* that had hit him when he saw her lose control.

And he didn't get scared. Not of anything.

But seeing her in that car, bleeding and unmoving, he couldn't seem to get to her fast enough.

Even now, as he stood awkwardly in the hall with her purse in his hand—which he'd gotten from her car before leaving the scene—waiting as he had been for the past hour, Kellan couldn't help but think about what might have happened had he *not* decided to follow her tonight.

The idea of Mia being stuck in that car, all alone and bleeding, scared with no way out... That shit tore him up in a way he didn't understand.

Other than the little bit of information Greyson had

discovered when he'd ran her plates last night, Kellan knew nothing about the woman. Yet the inexplicable pull he'd felt since she'd rear-ended him yesterday was stronger than ever.

And he had no idea why.

He'll find me.

Kellan ran a hand over the scruff covering his clenched jaw. The look of terror that had crossed over Mia's face when she'd said those words to him was like a knife to his gut.

It also conjured up a shitload of new questions.

Who was the *he* she'd been referring to? A partner in crime, maybe? An ex-lover? Someone Mia had wronged?

And why didn't she slow down for that curve?

There was an endless possibility of answers, and none that came to Kellan's mind were good. Then there was the way she'd responded to the one question he'd asked that he wished he could take back.

What did you do?

Fire and strength he didn't realize the mysterious woman possessed had cut through Mia's fear when she'd answered with a fierce, *I survived.*

Any semblance of doubt he'd had about the fact that she was in danger was obliterated with those two emotionally charged words. Now all Kellan could think about was finding out who she was hiding from and why.

Which reminded him...

He pulled his phone from his pocket and dialed Greyson's number. With the device to his ear, he watched a group of nurses walk by while he waited for his teammate to pick up.

Two rings later, he heard the former SEAL answer with a gruff, "Frost."

"It's me."

"McBride." Greyson's tone lifted a bit. "I was just about to call you."

Kellan's pulse kicked up. "You find something else?"

Before they left the bar last night, Greyson had gone out to his truck to run a preliminary check on Mia's plate. They'd gotten her last name, address, and date of birth.

Using that information, Kellan had waited until the guys were ready to leave Thirsty's before heading to Mia's for a solo stakeout. From his Jeep, he'd kept an eye out for any movement on her part. But once the final light went off in Mia's apartment, she'd remained inside for the rest of the night.

When he woke up at dawn with a kink in his neck and saw that her car still hadn't budged, he'd told himself he was crazy and headed home to sleep in an actual bed. But after tonight, after what she'd said to him, Kellan knew he wasn't crazy, after all.

"Your girl's clean," Greyson announced. "Sort of."

"Really?" That was a relief.

"From what I could find, for the past two years, Mia Carpenter has been a model citizen of the city of Richmond. She's single, no kids, pays her bills on time, and doesn't owe any back taxes. According to my search, she works from home as a freelance graphic arts designer."

Kellan had already searched through her purse, but the only things in there were her wallet, keys, phone, a pen, and a thing of lip balm. Her phone was set up with a password, which wasn't unusual these days, so he couldn't access it. Overall, nothing in there had jumped out at him as suspicious.

"Her record?" he asked his teammate.

"Clean as a whistle. The woman doesn't have so much as a parking ticket."

"You sure?"

"Are you seriously questioning my intel gathering abilities?"

"No." Kellan shook his head. "Look, I know this sounds crazy, but there's something going on with this woman. She's in some kind of trouble. I just don't know what."

The hospital's intercom was activated, blaring over the last of his words. A woman's voice came through the overhead speakers requesting the presence of one of the facility's doctors in the emergency department.

"You're at the hospital?" Greyson sounded worried. "What the hell happened? Are you okay?"

"I'm fine," Kellan quickly reassured his friend. "Mia was in a car accident a couple of hours ago. I'm standing outside her hospital room waiting for the doctor to finish up with her."

There was a slight pause and then, "How did you know she was in a wreck?"

"I was driving behind her when she hydroplaned."

Yeah, that didn't sound stalkerish in the least.

"You were tailing her?" Greyson's low curse came through the phone's speaker. "So let me get this straight. This Mia chick hits you yesterday, and then you just happen to be following her when she gets into another wreck tonight? Dude, what is it with this woman? You still pissed that she rear-ended your Jeep?"

"No, I'm not pissed," Kellan bit back. He'd never *been* pissed. More like intrigued. Glancing around to make sure no one could hear him, he lowered his voice to a hushed tone. "Look, I know it sounds crazy, but my gut is telling me she's in trouble. *Real* trouble. So, yeah. I staked out her place last night and again today. And it's a damn good thing, too.

Otherwise, she'd still be out in the storm, stuck in that fucking car all by herself."

Just thinking about it turned his stomach.

"Okay." His teammate took him at his word. "Well, if you really think this woman needs help you should talk to Winters. See if he'll agree to take her on as an official case."

"Not yet." Kellan turned his gaze to the closed door. "I don't want to bring this to Trace or the rest of the team until I know more."

Greyson waited a few seconds before responding. "I get that, but if something's going on with this woman—"

"Mia."

"Sorry. If something's going on with *Mia* that requires her protection, you need to figure out what the hell it is before we get called up for another assignment."

What Greyson was saying about bringing the entire team in to keep Mia safe made perfect sense. There was just one problem to that plan.

I want to be the one to protect her.

Kellan couldn't explain it, but the moment he'd stared into those gorgeous green eyes of hers, it was as if she'd become his responsibility. And somehow, in the last twenty-four hours, he'd become a man obsessed.

He was obsessed with finding out the truth about who she was hiding from. With figuring out how he could erase the fear she kept hidden in those emerald eyes.

He, he was obsessed with *her*.

But something Greyson said began tugging the back of his mind. "You said Mia was *sort of* clean. What did you mean by that?"

"I meant that for the past two years, Mia Carpenter has been a model citizen."

"And before that?"

"Before two years ago, the woman you know as Mia Carpenter didn't exist."

Fuck me. "She's using a fake name."

"That would be my guess."

"Can you—"

"Already got the program running, brother. I'm using West's facial recognition software to cross-match her Virginia driver's license photo with any missing persons reports or arrest warrants across the country. It might take some time, but we'll figure out who this woman...sorry, *Mia*...really is."

The man he was referring to was Derek West. Like Greyson, West was a former SEAL. He was also Alpha Team's technical analyst and a literal genius. As such, the man's patented facial rec program was the best of the best.

"Good," Kellan muttered. "Let me know what you find." The doctor chose that moment to come out of Mia's room, so he pushed himself off the wall and said, "I gotta go. Thanks for doing all this."

"Any time, brother." Greyson added, "I'll try to get some answers for you soon."

"Sounds good. Keep me posted." Kellan ended the call hoping to get those answers directly from the source. To the middle-aged doctor, he asked, "How's Mia?"

"I'm sorry, you are..."

Shit. His head had been filled with so many other things, he hadn't even thought about the whole HIPPA issue.

Knowing it was risky, Kellan schooled his expression and said, "I'm Kellan McBride. Mia and I are engaged."

"Well, Mr. McBride," the doctor didn't even question the claim. "Your fiancée is very lucky. No broken bones or internal injuries. She does have a concussion, but the tests we ran show that it's mild. We got her cleaned up, and I was able to stitch up the gash in her forehead. Thankfully, it's right next to her hairline, so once it heals, the scar will hardly be visible."

Kellan didn't care about the scar. He just wanted to see her.

"So, she's okay?"

"She's fine." He smiled. "She'll be sore for a few days and needs to take it easy. Miss Carpenter will also need to stay on top of the pain. I've written a prescription for a low-dose narcotic, but she can also use acetaminophen or ibuprofen if she prefers. Like I said, she's a very lucky young lady."

The relief Kellan felt from the doctor's report was much stronger than it should be, considering he and Mia had only just met. But that didn't make it any less real.

"Can I see her?"

"Sure." The other man nodded. "The nurse was helping her into a pair of clean scrubs since her clothes were covered in blood. They should be finished up by now."

"Thanks, Doc." He shook the man's hand.

"You can thank me by taking care of that fiancée of yours."

The man gave him a nod and went on his way.

For half a second, Kellan had the fleeting thought that he should probably feel guilty for deceiving the nice doctor. He didn't.

With a quick knock to the door, he waited for the all-clear before entering.

"Come in."

Her sweet voice was music to his ears.

"Hey." Kellan pushed the door wider and stepped inside.

Sitting with her legs dangling over the edge of the bed, Mia's round eyes widened with surprise when she saw him.

Wearing a set of clean, light blue scrubs, the blood from

before had been washed from her flawless skin and hair, and there was a small white bandage covering her new stitches.

"Perfect timing." The nurse with Mia flashed him a smile before turning back to her patient and asking, "This the guy you were telling me about? The one who called EMS to the scene?"

She's been talking about me?

"Yeah." Mia blushed. "That's Kellan."

"Lucky girl." The nurse winked at Mia playfully. To him, she said, "We're all done here. I'll go get Miss Carpenter's discharge papers, and then the two of you can be on your way."

"Thanks." Kellan stepped to the side to give the young woman room to walk past.

When they were alone, Mia stared at him with a look of confusion. "You're still here."

"Wasn't going to leave you here alone."

"Why not? It's not like we know each other."

"You're right. We don't." He stepped forward and handed her the purse. "I got this from your car. How are you feeling?"

"Thank you." She sounded relieved. "And I'm okay. Feels like my head's going to explode off my shoulders. But I'm still alive, so there's that."

Kellan's lips twitched. "They give you anything for pain? Because the doctor said he wrote a—"

"Are you the one who's been following me this past week?" The abrupt question stopped Kellan short. Alarm bells began ringing through his brain. "Someone's been following you?"

You know, other than me.

Because he'd only started watching her yesterday. If

someone else had been following her for the past week, then his instincts where she was concerned had to be spot on.

"Yes. Maybe." Mia grimaced. "I-I don't know. These past few days, I've had the feeling I'm being watched."

Gut feelings should never be ignored, but they'd come back to that later. First, he had to ask, "Why didn't you slow down before the curve?"

"I tried to, but my brakes wouldn't work."

Kellan frowned. "Not at all?"

"No. I even pulled the emergency brake, but nothing happened. Then my tires hit a puddle of water, and..." The memory had fresh tears glistening in her pretty eyes and her breath shaking. "Well, you were there. You know the rest."

"Have you had trouble with your brakes in the past?"

"No." She frowned. "I replaced the pads a few months ago, but other than them squeaking, I've never had an issue."

Not great news.

Kellan moved closer. He continued to press for as much information as he could get.

"You said you felt like someone's been watching you this past week. Any idea who?"

Mia's bow-shaped lips parted as if she were about to tell him, but then she cleared her throat and changed the subject.

"Look, I appreciate your interest with all of this...and your help after the wreck. But my head is pounding, and I really just want to call a cab so I can go home and go to bed."

Sliding off the mattress, she must've moved a little too quickly because the next thing Kellan knew, he was standing right in front of her. Grabbing her shoulders to keep her from falling to the floor.

"Easy there."

Small hands wrapped around his biceps, her delicate fingers digging into the sleeves of his black leather jacket. Despite the damp material serving as a barrier between them, Kellan had to force himself not to physically react from the jolt of electricity her touch created.

"Thanks." Mia looked everywhere but at him. "I guess I moved a little too quickly."

"Why don't you lay back down?" Kellan offered. "I'm sure the doc who treated you would agree to let you stay the night."

"He tried to get me to, actually. But I'm good. I just need to be more careful, that's all."

He doubted that, but it wasn't like he had any sort of claim on her. He could, however, offer to see her home.

"At least let me drive you home," Kellan offered.

Mia finally looked back up at him, and when she did, those gorgeous eyes of hers were filled with trepidation and mistrust.

"You never answered my question," she pointed out softly. "Why were you on that road tonight?"

"The truth?"

Mia nodded.

"I was following you."

The same fear from before flashed through her worried gaze, making Kellan want to kick his own ass for having caused it. She tried to move out of his arms, but he kept his grasp on her steady.

In a rush, he hurried to explain. "It's not what you think."

"Really?" Her chest heaved with frantic breaths.

"Because I think I just told you someone's been following me. Then I accidentally bump into you yesterday, and you admit to following me today."

Okay, so maybe it was exactly what she thought. But her reasoning as to why—whatever it was—had to be way off base.

"That's true," Kellan admitted. "But I wasn't following you because I want to hurt you."

"How do I know that? We only just met. For all I know, you could be working for—"

Mia cut herself short, and damn if Kellan didn't wish she hadn't.

"Working for who?"

"It doesn't matter." She slid out of his grasp and started for the door.

"It matters to me."

"Why?" She turned back around. "I mean, why are you even here, Kellan? Why do you care what happens to me?"

"Truth?" He asked for the second time in as many minutes. "I don't know. But if I wanted to hurt you, I would've done it when we were alone in the car. And I sure as hell wouldn't have called for an ambulance to bring you here. Yes, I was following you tonight, but you said you've felt eyes on you for the past week. That hasn't been me."

When Mia stared up at him with her adorable brow all furrowed and bunched with worry, Kellan found himself fighting the urge to reach out to her and soothe those lines away with his touch.

"Look, let's start over, okay?" he proposed. Taking a step back, he held out his hand for her to take. "My name is Kellan McBride. I'm an operative for a private security company here in Richmond, and one of the services we offer is protection. Yesterday, when we...bumped into each other...I got the feeling you might need some help in that department. So I had a guy on my team run your plate. That's how I was able to find you."

Her gaze fell to his outstretched hand, but Mia didn't take it. Instead, she looked back up at him with an incredulous expression. "You're trying to get me to *hire* you?"

"What?" Shit, he really was messing this whole thing up. "No," Kellan assured her, letting his hand drop back down to his side. "I'm not looking for anything other than to help you."

"What makes you think I need your help?"

With his gaze locked on hers, he rattled off a list of reasons. "You think someone's been following you for the past week. You ran your car into mine yesterday because something or someone caught your attention to the point you stopped watching where you were driving. And then tonight, you were damn near killed because your brakes went out. Brakes that you, yourself, claim have never been an issue before now."

"That could just be a coincidence."

"Maybe." Kellan stepped closer. "But in my experience, if your gut's telling you you're being watched, it's because you are."

The color in Mia's pretty face drained, and for a second, he was sure she was going to come clean. But then an invisible shield dulled the greens in her eyes, and she shut down.

"I'm not feeling well," she mumbled. "If you don't want to give me a ride home, then I'll call a—"

"I'll take you home, Mia." No way he was letting her take a fucking cab after what she'd been through. "It's not a problem."

Her guard was still up, but she gave him a soft, "Thank you."

The nurse returned with the discharge papers, a prescription for the pain medication to take as needed, and a wheelchair.

"Is that really necessary?" Mia eyed the chair.

"Sorry, Miss Carpenter. It's hospital policy. With a head injury like yours, you could get dizzy and fall, and then we'd be on the hook for any further injuries you may occur."

"Come on, sweetheart." Kellan rested his hand on her back and guided her to the chair. "I'll push you to the entrance, and then I'll go grab my car and bring it around to the front."

Without argument, Mia did as he asked and settled into the wheelchair. With her purse and the paperwork clutched in her lap, she spoke softly to the nurse when she said, "Thank you."

"Take care of yourself." The other woman wore a genuine smile. "And remember what I said. If your symptoms worsen or you start feeling dizzy or out of sorts, come back and see us."

"Okay."

"You ready?" Kellan stared down at Mia and waited.

When she gave him a slight nod, he said goodbye to the kind nurse and pushed Mia down the hall and to the emergency department's entrance.

"I'll be right back," he promised as he positioned the wheelchair off to the side of the doors.

"I'll be here."

Kellan nearly smiled at the woman's smart-assed tone. He couldn't really blame her for being grumpy after the night she'd had.

Walking through the automated doors, he was hit with a rush of cold, damp air. The rain had stopped, which was a blessing all on its own, but in the wake of the storm, the already-cool December temperature had dropped several degrees.

Holy fuck, it's cold.

Kellan pulled his jacket closed, wishing he'd had the aforethought to start the Jeep sooner. Sliding his hand into his pocket, he pressed the button on his large fob twice; the telltale honking of his horn letting him know the vehicle's engine had started.

Located in the heart of Richmond, the VCU Medical Center was the highest-rated hospital in the city. Something that should've put his mind at ease when it came to Mia's care and discharge.

But it didn't.

He wanted her to stay in the hospital overnight. At least that way, she wouldn't be alone.

For a minute, he'd even considered offering to stay with her. But given her apprehensiveness toward him giving her a ride home, he knew without asking that letting him crash on her couch would be out of the question.

Not that he could blame her for that, either. They didn't know each other, and he'd already admitted to following her. From what Greyson had told him, she was single and lived alone. So no, she *shouldn't* invite a strange man into her apartment for an overnight stay.

But that didn't make him wish for it any less.

Finally reaching his Jeep, Kellan grabbed the handle which automatically unlocked the doors. He hopped inside, blasting the heat as high as it could go, and pressed the button to get the passenger seat heated up, as well.

The last thing Mia needed was to have to ride home on freezing cold leather.

Making his way through the massive parking lot, Kellan pulled under the canopy covering the emergency department's entrance. With the engine running, he got out and went back inside to where Mia was waiting for him.

"Here." He slid his jacket from his shoulders and wrapped it around hers. "You're going to need that."

"O-okay." She pulled the top of the garment together with her fists. "Thank you."

Barely resisting the urge to reach for her, Kellan positioned himself behind the chair and grabbed the padded handles. "Let's get you home."

Without another word, Kellan pushed Mia through the sliding doors and out to his Jeep. He helped her climb inside before returning the wheelchair. Then he proceeded to drive her home.

Since he already knew where she lived, he didn't have to ask for directions. Good thing, since she spent the entire ride with her head rested back against the seat and her eyes closed.

Stopping at the pharmacy closest to her apartment, Kellan was thankful it was a 24-hour kind of place. Otherwise, she'd have to wait until morning to get her pain meds filled.

Since it was late, and they weren't busy, it didn't take but a few minutes for her prescription to be filled. Mia had given him her insurance card, but when she tried to pay the bill, he waved her away and handed the pharmacist his credit card.

As they drove away, Mia sounded almost mad when she told him, "You didn't have to do that."

"I know."

"I don't understand you." She settled back against her seat.

"That's okay." Kellan turned onto the street leading to her complex. "Most people don't."

"Yeah, well, in my experience, most people don't help strangers simply out of the goodness of their hearts, either."

The comment turned his gut. "Sounds like you've been hanging around the wrong kinds of people."

"You have no idea." Mia scoffed. "Well, that used to be the case, anyway."

"Not anymore?"

"Nope." Her hair swished against the leather as she shook her head. "Not anymore."

Kellan pushed back the urge to press her further. She was hurting and tired and needed to rest. He might be dropping her off tonight, but he'd be checking in with her again tomorrow.

His questions could wait until then.

"We're here." He pulled into the closest available parking spot. "Stay put. I'll come help you down."

Pushing the button to cut the engine, he got out and walked around the back of the Jeep to the passenger side. Opening the door for her, Kellan took her purse and papers before gently taking hold of her hand and guiding her down onto her feet.

Like before, they both became lost in a sort of trance as they stared back at each other with an interest he couldn't explain. A cool breeze blew past, and once again, their strange connection was broken.

"Let's get you inside."

"I can manage from here."

"I'm sure you can, but I'm still walking you to your door. Come on." He rested a hand against her lower back, keeping it there as they made their way to Mia's apartment door.

She was on the ground floor, which for security purposes wasn't great. But the fact that she didn't have to climb a bunch of stairs after sustaining a head injury wasn't necessarily a bad thing.

The way the apartments were set up, there was a covered walkway between each building. Mia's apartment was the last one on the left of her walkway, and he couldn't help but wonder if that was a purposeful choice on her part.

Back in the corner, away from the complex's main traffic.

If he were trying to hide from someone and had chosen to live here, that's the apartment he would've chosen, too.

Mia dug her keys from her purse. "I know it probably doesn't seem like it, but I really do appreciate your help tonight."

"I'm just glad I was there." Kellan held out his hand palm up. "Why don't you let me check out the place before I leave. Just to make sure it's clear."

Her round eyes blinked as she looked back at the closed door. "You think someone's in there?"

"I think I won't sleep tonight if I leave here without knowing for sure."

"Okay." She handed him the keys.

Unlocking the doors, he pulled his gun from the holster positioned at the back of his waistband. When Mia's adorable mouth fell open, he quickly reassured her.

"I always carry. It's part of the job."

"Security expert." She swallowed. "Right."

"I'm sure everything's fine, but I want you to stay just inside the door while I clear the apartment. Just in case."

"O-okay."

Damn, he hated the tremor in her voice. Especially since he'd caused it. But he wasn't lying.

There was no way in hell he'd get a wink of sleep if he didn't make sure her place was secure before leaving.

Door open, Kellan flipped on the light switch to his left

and swept the immediate area. The living room came first, and it took all of two seconds to see that it was clear. To his right was a small dining area just outside a modest, semi-open kitchen.

Once those were checked, Kellan made his way down a small hallway, checking a linen closet on his left and a full bath to his right. Then he opened the door at the end of the hall and found himself standing in Mia's bedroom.

Soft and feminine, it suited her perfectly. Hints of lavender and vanilla hung in the air, the same scent he'd picked up the day before when they'd first met.

Her bed was the focal point of the room, and had been made with crisp, clean lines. Beside that was a nightstand and positioned in the corner of the room was a computer desk and black leather chair.

The place seemed immaculate compared to his. Not that he was a slob. But from what Kellan was seeing, Mia kept her living space extremely neat and tidy.

Ignoring the bed and the images it threatened to create, he continued doing his thing until every nook and cranny of the apartment had been checked.

"Looks good." He holstered his weapon as he made his way back to her. "You have a nice place."

"Thanks." She offered him a tiny smile.

"You have your meds, right?"

"In here." Mia patted her purse. "I was going to try to hold off taking anything, but there's a congo band taking up residence in my head, so I think I'll take one before I go to bed."

"Good." He hated the thought of her hurting. "You'll want to stay on top of the pain. Don't wait until it gets too bad, because then it's twice as hard to get under control."

"You sound like you're talking from experience."

"I am."

There was a stretch of awkward silence before she slid his jacket from her shoulders and handed it back to him. "Here." She handed it to him and then held out her hand. "Thanks again, Kellan. For everything."

His large hand engulfed hers. "You're welcome." Though he hated to let her go, Kellan released his hold and grabbed his wallet from his back pocket. Pulling out his business card, he said, "I want you to keep this with you. You have any trouble or need anything, call that number. Actually... do you have a pen in there?" He motioned to her purse.

He knew she did but didn't want her knowing he'd searched through her things earlier.

"Um...yeah. I think so." Mia dug around and pulled it out. "Here."

"Thanks," Kellan mumbled as he turned the card over. Scribbling his personal number on the back, he handed her the card and the pen. "That's my cell on the back. Just call that number if you need anything. Day or night."

She ran her thumb across the embossed R.I.S.C. on the front. "You really work for this company?"

"I do."

"I want to believe you." Mia's throat worked as she swallowed hard, her eyes still glued to that damn card. "I want to be able to trust...someone."

"You can trust me."

She lifted her gaze to his, the uncertainty there damn near breaking him. "I wish that were true."

"Sweetheart, if you're in trouble, I promise you, I can help you."

"You can't." She shook her head. "No one can."

A single tear fell from the corner of her eye, and Kellan had the sudden urge to wipe it away. Giving in, he started to reach out for her, but Mia flinched away from the impending contact.

And there it was.

Hidden before, Kellan now understood what had caused that nagging feeling in his gut the second he first saw her. He finally recognized the source of the terror reflected back at him through her emerald gaze.

It was a look he recognized all-too-well because he'd seen it before.

As a child, Kellan had faced that very same look time and time again. It was the same horrified expression his mother used to wear when his father would come home in one of his moods.

A mood that typically ended with Kellan hiding under his bed and his mother bleeding and bruised. The same mood that had sent his mother to the grave and his piece of shit dad to prison.

That same experience was the reason Kellan knew that this woman, whoever she really was, wasn't afraid of *him*. She was terrified of the person who used to hurt her.

The same person who'd sent her running to his city two years ago.

"Who is he, Mia?" Kellan did his best not to growl the question. "Who hurt you?"

Mia blinked, sending twin tears streaming down her flushed cheeks. With her watery gaze meeting his once more, she finally gave him a piece of the truth.

"My husband."

Son of a bitch.

Kellan's stomach bottomed out. "Can't you call the cops? I'm sure they could help you with—"

"The cops." She started laughing; the sound holding no

semblance of humor. "That might work for some women, but not for me."

"Why not?"

"Because my husband *is* a cop. And if he ever finds me... he'll kill me."

4

MIA WOKE the next morning with a headache from hell and tenderness in muscles she didn't even know she had. The doctor had warned her she'd be sore, but damn. She couldn't remember the last time she felt this sore.

Yes, you do.

Her subconscious was right. Though she hardly thought about it anymore, the last time Mia woke up feeling this out-of-sorts was the morning after she'd left her old life to come here.

Pushing those pointless thoughts away, she threw the covers off and made her way to the bathroom. After a shower that consisted of her keeping the water away from her stitches, she got dressed in a pair of ripped jeans and a white, long-sleeve t-shirt.

Forgoing socks for her fuzzy slippers, she threw her hair into a messy bun and went in search of pain meds and some much-needed caffeine. As she waited for the coffee to brew, she spotted the card Kellan had given her last night lying on the counter. She picked it up and read the wording again.

. . .

R.I.S.C., Inc.
Private Security Specialists

There was a downtown address, a phone number, and email printed in the bottom left corner. Flipping it over, she ran her thumb across the handwritten number Kellan had penned before handing the card to her.

Frustrated with herself for opening up to him the way she had, Mia started to shake her head but stopped when the action sent a shockwave of pain through her skull.

"If this is a mild concussion, I'd hate to see what a major one feels like," she mumbled to herself as she slid onto one of her two barstools.

Setting the card down in front of her, Mia thought about the conversation she and Kellan had shared before he left. She still couldn't believe she'd told him—a man she barely knew—about Elliot. Sure, she hadn't gone into detail, but by the way he'd looked at her and the things he'd said after, she hadn't needed to.

He already knew.

There was so much more to her story than what little she'd shared, but it wasn't anything she cared to tell anyone. Especially not a man who'd already admitted to following her around.

If he hadn't, who knows what would've happened to you down in that ravine.

Kellan claimed to be one of the good guys, and so far, he hadn't given her any reason to doubt that. He'd gotten her help after the wreck, stayed with her the entire time at the hospital, and then driven her home *and* made sure her apartment was safe.

All for a woman he barely knew.

But then there was the look he'd given her when she'd been stupid enough to run her mouth about her past. It was the same pitying expression the people of Denning, North Carolina always gave her when she passed them on the sidewalk or stood next to them in line at the grocery store.

Because everyone in that town knew the truth. They were simply too afraid to do anything to help.

It wasn't their fault, though. Not really. When a man like Elliot Devereaux was the sheriff, and that same man's influential family owned half the town, there wasn't a whole lot anyone could do.

You could've done more. You could've aired your dirty laundry all over town. Tried to get Elliot fired. Filed for divorce instead of running away like a coward.

A ringing phone broke up the solo pity party she'd apparently decided to throw for herself. Walking back to her bedroom, Mia grabbed her phone from the charging station on her nightstand and looked at the screen.

Unknown Caller.

It wasn't unusual to get those, given that very few people had her number. In fact, the only contacts saved in her phone were her clients and former brother-in-law. And she only kept his number in there in case of an emergency.

Thinking about Shane added to Mia's melancholy mood. She missed talking to him. He always seemed to make her laugh.

But holding onto *any* part of her old life was too dangerous a game. One she refused to be a part of anymore.

The phone rang again, and Mia found herself hoping it was Kellan. Maybe he was calling to check on her?

You won't know until you answer the damn phone.

"Shit." Sliding her thumb across the screen, Mia answered the incoming call. "Hello?" She was met with nothing but silence. "Hello?" she repeated, but still there was no response.

After trying a third time, she decided it was either a bad connection or a wrong number and ended the call. With her phone in hand, she went back into the kitchen to find the biggest coffee mug in her cabinet.

Halfway there, the phone began to ring again. Like before, it was an unknown caller. And like before, when she answered, there was no one there.

Refusing to let it upset her, Mia set the phone down and grabbed her favorite mug. After pouring in just the right amount of Italian sweet cream creamer into the cup, she filled it to the rim with steaming liquid she'd always swore was a magical gift from God.

A quick stir with her spoon and she was taking that first glorious sip. Letting out an audible moan, Mia closed her eyes and savored the rich, smooth flavor.

Her phone began ringing again.

"Seriously?" Getting agitated, Mia kept her mug in one hand and answered the phone with the other. "Look, I don't know who you are, but if you're not going to talk, then—"

"Hello, Mia."

Her lungs froze and her stomach dropped.

No. It can't be him. It can't be!

"I've missed you."

"W-who is this?"

A tsk hit her ear before she heard, "Come now. Has it been so long, you've forgotten the sound of your own husband's voice?"

The mug fell from Mia's hand. Shards of porcelain scattered across the ceramic tile floor as hot liquid splashed around her feet. Ending the call, Mia dropped the phone onto the counter.

The world spun all around her. Fear turned the blood in her veins to ice, and she couldn't seem to catch her breath.

He'd found her. Despite all her efforts to the contrary, the man who'd taken everything from her had *found* her.

Oh, God.

The phone began ringing again, snapping her out of the terror-induced trance. With trembling fingers, she picked up the phone once more, nearly dropping it in the process. Pressing the button on the side, she sent the call to voicemail as she searched for an answer as to what she should do next.

Think, Mia. You need to think.

Catching a glimpse of Kellan's card, she fumbled to pick it up from the slick countertop. Without another thought, she started to dial the number he'd written on the back when those same seven digits appeared on her screen.

"Kellan?" She hated the way her voice shook.

"Hey." There was a slight pause and then, "I was calling to see how you were feeling."

Better, now that I'm talking to you. "He called me."

"Who?"

"My husband."

There was a slight pause before he asked, "The one you told me about last night?"

"Yes."

"When?"

"Just now. I-I don't know how he got my number, but—"

"You sure it was him?"

"I was married to the man for three years, Kellan. I know his voice."

She'd never forget the sound of the man who'd destroyed her life.

"Okay, sweetheart. I believe you."

Mia let out a shaky breath. "If he figured out my phone number, it's only a matter of time before he finds me. I-I don't know what to do."

"You're not going to do anything."

"But—"

"Listen to me, Mia. I'm on my way to you right now, okay? I want you to make sure your door and windows are locked, and then I want you to stay inside until I get there. I'll be at your place in less than ten. Do not open the door for anyone else but me, got it?"

"O-okay."

"I know it's hard but try to relax."

Relax. Right.

Sensing her uncertainty, Kellan added a soft, "We're going to figure this out, sweetheart. I promise."

That he'd said *we* eased the tension in her muscles slightly. "Thank you."

"I'll see you soon."

As promised, Kellan was knocking on her door less than ten minutes later. Checking the peephole to make sure it was him, Mia rushed to unlock both locks before flinging the door open and throwing herself into his arms.

It was a move she hadn't meant to make, but it felt good, all the same.

"Thanks for coming."

His strong arms wrapped around her, holding her close. "Jesus, Mia. You're shaking like a leaf."

"Sorry." She started to pull back, but he wrapped his fingers around her shoulders and held her in place.

"You don't apologize for being scared. Not ever, you understand?"

Mia nodded with a whispered, "Okay."

"Grab your things," he ordered. "I'm taking you to my office."

"And then what?"

His gaze locked with hers, the grays of his eyes swirling with fierce determination. "Then you and I are going to figure out our next move."

Again, he spoke as if it were the two of them against the world. Mia was cautious not to get too wrapped up in what any of it meant. She'd done that once before, and it was that decision that brought her to where she was now.

Still, for the first time in a very long while, Mia felt as though she wasn't alone.

***

Less than an hour later, she was sitting at the far end of a large table in the center of a conference room. Surrounded by five of the best looking, well-built men she'd ever seen.

But only one made her heart skip a beat.

"Mia Carpenter, this is Trace Winters, our team leader." Kellan pointed to the man sitting at the table's end.

Trace greeted her with a nod of his salt-and-peppered head. "Pleasure to meet you, Ms. Carpenter."

Giving him a small smile, Mia glanced at each of the other men as Kellan introduced them.

"To Trace's right is Asher Cross, our sniper."

The dark-haired man smiled, looking much too young to be on a team such as this. But if he was here, Mia figured there must be a reason.

"Next to him is our demolitions and computer guru, Greyson Frost." Kellan pointed to a large, muscular man with hair that went past his shoulders.

Something struck a chord, and Mia stared back at the

man who could be Jason Momoa's brother. "You're the one Kellan told me about. The one who ran my license plate."

"Guilty as charged." The man's deep voice rumbled. He was big, burly, and intimidating as hell. But there was a kindness in his unusual golden eyes that put her at ease.

"And last but not least is Rhys Maddox." Kellan motioned to the tall, dark, and ruggedly handsome man to her left. "Rhys is Charlie Team's medic."

"Hi." Mia gave the group a half-wave. Because how else did a woman in her position greet a room full of alpha bodyguard types?

"Ms. Carpenter—"

"Devereaux," Mia corrected the man in charge.

It had been two years since she'd used that name, and it felt foreign on her tongue. But she'd chosen to put her life in this team's hands, which meant coming clean about…everything.

"I'm sorry?" Trace frowned.

With a quick sideways glance at Kellan, Mia pulled her shoulders back and told them the truth. "My real name is Mia Devereaux. Carpenter was my grandmother's maiden name. But you can just call me Mia."

"All right then, Mia." Trace's lips curved into a half-smile. "Why don't you tell us why you're here."

She let out a slow breath. "It's kind of a long story. I don't even know where to start."

"How about the beginning?" His smile grew a tiny bit. "And take your time. There's no rush."

With Kellan's supportive nod, Mia drew in a steeling breath and told them the whole embarrassing, ugly truth.

"My parents and I moved to Denning, North Carolina when I was fifteen. My dad got a job working for an automotive factory near there. Anyway, I was a freshman, and Elliot

Devereaux was a senior. At the time, he didn't even know I existed, but he was every teenage girl's dream. Good looking, captain of the football team, and he was the youngest in the town's most affluential family."

"What made his family so important?"

"Elliot's parents own the largest real estate company in Warren County. In turn, they own half the buildings in Denning."

"So they literally own half the town."

"Exactly." Mia nodded. "Anyway, Elliot graduated high school and went away to college. By the time I was out of school and starting college, he'd graduated with a degree in criminal justice and was hired with the sheriff's department."

"When did you and Devereaux hook up?"

"My senior year in college. In the years before that, we'd run into each other here and there when I'd come back to visit my parents or stay during the school's extended holiday breaks. At the time, we were just friends. Elliot had gotten married to his high school sweetheart right after he was hired on as a deputy."

There was a break in conversation before Greyson said, "So you and Devereaux were..."

"Friends." Mia knew where he was headed, and she quickly cut him off at the pass. "Elliot and I were never more than friends until after his wife died."

Rhys turned his dark eyes onto her. "How'd she die?"

"ATV accident on their land." Mia didn't know the details, just that Elliot and Katie Jo had been out riding on a Sunday afternoon when tragedy struck. "From what I heard at the time, his wife lost control of her four-wheeler and ran it into a tree."

"So the guy loses his wife, and you decide to slide on in?"

"What the hell, Maddox?" Kellan scowled at his teammate.

"Sorry." Rhys put his hands up defensively. "Just trying to get the whole picture."

"It's okay." Mia turned to Rhys. "It's an easy assumption to make, but no. I didn't *slide* into anything. Like I said, Elliot and I were friends long before we started dating."

"And when was that, exactly?"

The question came from Trace.

"I came home from college to attend Katie's funeral with my parents. The whole town was there, but Elliot seemed so alone and distraught. I felt bad for him and wanted to help in any way I could, so I gave him my number before I left." She quickly added, "*Only* as a friend. I told him to call me if he needed someone to talk to."

"Let me guess..." Rhys continued his bad cop routine, "You two quickly became more than friends."

"If you consider a year quick, then sure." Mia held her own with the untrusting man. "Because that's how long it took before anything romantic ever happened between us."

"It's okay, Mia." Kellan put a gentle hand on her forearm. "No one here is judging you."

Tell that to Mr. Personality over here.

"Go on, Mia," Trace prompted. "Tell us why you split town and started a new life under a fake name, and why you're so scared of your estranged husband."

"After my college graduation, I moved back to Denning. I have a Bachelor's in graphic arts, and that got me hired on with the yearbook publishing company there in town. It wasn't until then that Elliot and I'd begun dating. At first, everything was great."

"What changed?" The man named Asher finally spoke up.

"We got married." Mia looked at him from across the table. "We'd been dating nine months when he proposed." She remembered feeling like the luckiest woman in the world the day she became Elliot Devereaux's wife. "Shortly after, he became the youngest man ever elected sheriff of Warren County. Between the wedding and all the election events, those first few months flew by. Like I said, things were good, but then something...changed." Elliot changed.

"How so?"

"I honestly don't even know how it happened. Things started out small, I guess. The more time passed, the more controlling Elliot became." Controlling and possessive. "Little by little, he managed to isolate me from my friends and co-workers. My parents. And when they were killed in an automobile accident a year later, Elliot and his family were all I had left. It was like... One day I woke up and had no idea who I was anymore."

A few seconds of silence passed before Kellan asked, "When did the abuse start?"

Mia glanced down at her hands, which were rested on the table in front of her. Balling them up, she focused on those as she told them this next part.

"About six months into the marriage. It was only verbal at first, but it wasn't long before he started to hit. Sometimes it was because he would drink too much after a long day at work. Other times, I'd simply say or do the wrong thing and set him off."

"Tell us about two years ago, when you left Denning to come to Richmond," Trace commanded.

Mia's eyes rose to his. "How do you know it's been two years?"

"That would be me." Greyson raised his hand. "When I dug a little deeper after running your plates, could find no record of a Mia Carpenter living in Richmond before then."

Computer genius. Right. Of course.

"Things with Elliot had gotten pretty bad by year three. I was constantly walking on eggshells, carefully considering every word that came out of my mouth before I spoke it. But that night..." She forced herself to face those awful memories. "That night it didn't seem to matter what I did. One minute I was in the kitchen finishing up dinner and asking him about his day, and the next, I was being thrown down the front steps of our house."

Kellan's entire body stiffened beside her, and before she realized it, he'd reached over and covered her fists with one of his own.

"It's okay, sweetheart." He spoke with the gentlest of tones. "You don't have to go on."

Actually, she did.

"I've never told anyone this story." She looked over at him. "Or any of the others, for that matter. But it's time someone knows the truth about Elliot Devereaux."

"Like I said, Mia," Trace chimed in. "We're in no hurry."

Offering the formidable man a small smile, Mia went on.

"I was laying on those steps that night, crying and holding a broken arm when Elliot put his gun to the back of my head and threatened to pull the trigger."

Letting out a low curse, Kellan squeezed her hand and held on tight. It was almost as if the thought of losing her was unbearable, which of course, it wasn't. Not for him, anyway.

Elliot, on the other hand...

"I thought he was going to kill me that night." Mia lifted her chin. "And frankly, a big part of me wanted him to."

"If you were dead, he couldn't hurt you anymore." Kellan's knowing gaze reached deep into her soul.

There was no judgement or pity in his eyes this time around. Only acceptance and something resembling heartache.

The former sent a shockwave of relief through her system. The latter only made her more confused. But one thing she felt to her core was that he somehow understood.

"Exactly." Mia nodded. "It's why I chose to leave rather than file for divorce. Elliot told me a long time ago he'd kill me before he ever let me walk away."

Dark emotion swirled behind tormented eyes as he stared back at her, confusing her even more than she already was.

Why would this man—pretty much still a stranger at this point—have such an emotional reaction to her pain? It wasn't like they were friends or lovers.

But wouldn't it be nice if you were?

Mia shook the thought away. The last thing she needed was to get romantically involved with someone. She was technically still married, for crying out loud.

Even so, she barely remembered what it was like to have a friend. Someone she could count on to always be there. A person she trusted who would be there when she called. Someone to offer her a shoulder to cry on, or a hand to hold.

You can count on Kellan.

She glanced down at their joined hands and forced back the tears threatening to fall. She wanted to believe that with all her heart, but there was a time when Elliot had held her hand like this, too. A time she never would've believed in a million years that he would hurt her.

And look at how that turned out.

Pulling her hand free, Mia sat up straight and finished the rest of her pathetic story.

"After Elliot left the house that night, I used a burner phone to call his brother. Shane had long suspected what was going on, but he didn't dare go up against family. Not publicly, anyway. A few months before, he'd caught me alone at one of their family dinners. He could tell something was off and begged me to let him help. But I knew what Elliot would do to the both of us if I did, so I stayed...until that awful night three months later."

"So after Elliot left the house, you called your brother-in-law to come get you?" Asher asked with genuine curiosity.

"I called him, yes." Mia nodded. "But Shane met me at the old grain bins just outside of town. He'd somehow gotten me a used car with plates belonging to Mia Carpenter from Richmond. He also had a driver's license with my picture and new last name, and he'd secured the apartment I live in now. Even paid the first six months' rent to buy me time to find a job and start making my own money again."

Because once they were married, Elliot had insisted she not work. Which, in hindsight, should've been her first clue as to the man's narcissistic tendencies.

"I'm curious." Rhys rested his elbows on the table. "Why would your husband's brother help you?"

"Because Shane isn't like the others in his family. He's a decent and kind man who helped others whenever he could."

"Yet he stood by while his brother beat the shit out of his sister-in-law."

Mia met Rhys's doubting gaze. "Only because I asked him to. After what happened that night with Elliot, I knew if he ever found out Shane had helped me disappear, Elliot would kill us both. And he'd get away with it, too."

"Because he's the sheriff?" Greyson asked.

Mia slid her gaze to his and nodded. "And a Devereaux."

Asher spoke up again when he said, "Surely someone else knew what the bastard was doing to you."

"Oh, they knew." She smiled sadly. "But Elliot and his family also knew everyone else's dirty little secrets. The people of Denning didn't dare speak a negative word about the Devereaux's for fear of retribution."

"What about medical records?" Rhys asked. "If he hurt you the way you claim, there should be some sort of—"

"He *did* hurt me, Mr. Maddox." Mia needed to make that point very clear. "But like I said, the people in that town are in the Devereaux's pockets. Including the only doctor in the area."

"Let me guess." Greyson spoke up again. "He made house calls?"

"Frequently, I'm afraid." She sighed. "You see, Dr. Conners has a bit of an opioid problem. He uses and deals. In exchange for his discretion when his services were needed, Elliot agreed to look the other way and let the good doctor continue with his side business."

"Jesus." Asher's dark brows turned inward. "What the hell kind of town is this?"

Mia shared a look with the young sniper as she said, "The kind you never want to live in."

"Okay, so we have a pretty detailed account of what brought you to Virginia." Trace regained control of the room. "What about recent events? When McBride set up this meeting, he mentioned something about a phone call?"

Kellan cleared his throat beside her. "I called Mia earlier to see how she was feeling after her rollover accident last night."

All eyes turned to her, and she absentmindedly brushed her fingers against the bandage covering her wound. "My brakes went out on my way home from the store last night. It was storming, and I hydroplaned on a sharp curve."

"Your brakes just...went out?" Rhys frowned. "Had you been having issues with them prior to last night?"

It was the same question Kellan had asked.

"No." She shook her head. "They've never given me any problems."

Kellan continued. "When I called Mia earlier, she sounded really upset. Said Devereaux had just called her."

"How'd he get your number?" Rhys asked. "I'm assuming you left your old phone behind when you split town?"

Mia confirmed his assumption. "I did, and I've been using the burner phone Shane gave me ever since. I honestly have no idea how he got that number."

"Is it possible his brother gave it to him?"

Asher's question made her chuckle. "No. There's no way Shane would've given Elliot the number. Not after all the trouble he went through to help me get away."

"And you're certain it was your husband who called?" Trace looked back at her.

"It was him." Of that, Mia had no doubt.

Shifting in his chair beside her, Kellan faced her more directly. "What did he say when he called?"

"That he missed me." Everything had happened so fast, they hadn't had much time to talk about it before now.

"And what did you say in return?" Trace spoke up again.

"Nothing. As soon as I realized who it was, I hung up. The phone rang a few more times, but I ignored it. Then Kellan called, and...here we are."

Trace waited a beat before pushing himself to his feet. "I think we have enough for now. We'll need to learn a bit more before deciding to take the case, but I'll let you know our decision as soon as possible."

Mia's stomach dropped as she turned to Kellan. "I thought you said you could help me."

"I will." He eyed his other teammates. "We just need some time to find out as much as we can about your husband."

"Meaning, you need to check out my story to see if I'm telling the truth."

"It's procedure, Mrs. Devereaux," Trace attempted to appease her.

"Please don't call me that." Mia muttered low. "I know on paper, Elliot and I are still married, but beyond that...I don't ever want to be called that name again."

"Understood." Trace looked at Greyson. "Start digging. Let me know what you find."

"You got it, Boss." The long-haired man stood, and the others followed his lead.

"What about me?" Mia looked around the room. "What do I do in the meantime?"

"In the meantime..." Trace thought for a moment. "I'd like Kellan to stay with you. If your husband's the man you say he is, and he is in town, I don't want to risk him showing up with you unprotected."

"I can sleep on your couch," Kellan added. "But only if you're comfortable with that. If not, I can watch your place from my car."

Like he'd apparently already been doing.

"You can take the couch." Mia told him.

She couldn't very well let him sleep in his car while he was doing her a favor. After all, it was getting colder and more wintery every day.

Sure, keep telling yourself that's the reason you're letting this handsome hunk of a man stay with you.

Ignoring the inappropriate thought, Mia gave the group a final glance of appreciation. "Thank you." She met each man's gaze. "Even if you decide not to take my case, I appreciate you having taken the time to listen."

Greyson was the one to respond. "As we were talking, I pulled up some basic intel on Devereaux and sent it to McBride." He tapped the screen on his tablet and looked back up at them. "I should have the rest of what I need by tonight."

Man, he really *was* good. "Okay."

"Until then, McBride, I want you to stick close to Mia." Trace ordered. "Just in case."

"Don't worry." A rush of unexpected heat reached out to her from Kellan's determined gaze. He didn't look at anyone else as he said, "I won't let her out of my sight."

5

This isn't one of your better ideas.

The annoying voice in Kellan's head was probably right. Sleeping under the same roof as Mia may not be the wisest decision he'd ever made, but he couldn't bring himself to suggest something less tempting like a hotel with adjoining rooms.

So here he was, in his bedroom packing an overnight bag while she waited for him in his living room.

Wonder what she thinks of the place?

The thought caught Kellan off guard. Her opinion of his apartment shouldn't matter. It wasn't like they were dating or anything. But Mia *was* the first woman to ever be here

As a rule, Kellan didn't invite women back to his apartment. On the off chance that he connected with someone on a physical basis—which hadn't happened in much longer than he cared to admit—they'd usually go to her place. After a couple hours of fun, they'd say their goodbyes, and he'd come back here.

Alone.

But tonight was different. This wasn't about romance or sex. It was about keeping Mia safe and nothing more.

So why are you so worried about what she thinks?

"I'm not," he mumbled to himself.

Great. Now he was talking to himself. What the fuck was happening to him?

Ignoring the question—because he damn sure wasn't ready to face the answer—Kellan finished tossing a few essentials into his bag and left the room.

As he went in search of his unexpected guest, he noted that his apartment was clean and tidy, and the basics were all there. Living room, kitchen, bathroom, two bedrooms, although one was his office... But as he made his way back into the living room, he realized for the first time just how blah his home really was.

Suddenly, Kellan found himself wishing he'd put more thought into decorating.

The woman's crazy-ass husband is fucking with her. I seriously doubt she's worried about the lack of throw pillows or the color of your bath towels.

Keeping that in mind, Kellan cleared his head of the pointless line of thinking and focused on what truly mattered.

Mia.

Standing in front of the floating shelf mantel positioned over his living room's sleek, modern gas fireplace, Mia's back was to him as she glanced over the handful of framed photos aligning the stained wood.

He watched silently as one by one, she studied them.

In them, Kellan was a few years younger. And in each one, he was dressed in military camouflage.

"Those are from my Marine days," he rumbled from behind.

Startled, Mia turned and looked at him from over her shoulder. The smile she wore was like a soothing balm to his damaged soul, which only furthered his confusing feelings toward her.

"You were in the Marines?" she asked softly.

"I was." Kellan carried a black duffle toward her. "Got out after my last tour overseas and was hired on with RISC shortly after."

"Thank you for your service."

A strange warmth spread across his chest. "It was my pleasure."

Looking back at one of the pictures, Mia picked it up and ran her fingertips across the glass. In it, his beard was full and his skin dust and sweat-covered.

Grinning, he remembered the frozen moment in time. He'd been goofing off with his former unit, the other guys laughing and smiling right along with him.

"That was a good day," he commented. One of a few from that last trip overseas.

Mia carefully set the frame back in its rightful place. "Do you miss it?"

"Some parts, I do. Others…not so much." He came closer, stopping when he was right next to her. "With Charlie Team, I get to do a lot of the same things I did for Uncle Sam, only without all the red tape and pencil pushers telling us what we can't do."

That shit got unbelievably frustrating when all they wanted to do was take down the threats to the U.S. while protecting and/or rescuing the innocent. Working for RISC, he and his new team were able to focus on what was truly important, rather than all the political BS.

"Do you think your team will let me hire them?" The hope in her words was damn near palpable.

"I don't know," he answered her honestly. "Either way, I won't stop protecting you. Not until I know you're safe."

Eyes he wanted to get lost in stared back at him, and when Kellan locked his gaze with hers, he could no longer deny the connection he felt to this woman.

He wasn't sure what any of it meant, but deep down, he knew one thing with utter certainty.

I want her.

He didn't understand how it had happened or when. Hell, he'd only known her two whole days.

But what Kellan *did* know was that his desire for the woman standing inches away was the strongest, most powerful need he'd felt in a long damn time. And regardless of the timing, it was very, *very* real.

Too bad he couldn't act on it.

Kellan had never even considered being with a married woman, but that wasn't what was holding him back with Mia. If even half of what she'd said about her asshole husband was true, that prick gave up any claim to her the second he laid a hand on her in anger.

No, what kept him from making move in that direction was the fact that she was a client. Or rather, an almost-client. Either way, his job was to protect her, not try to bed her.

So, he shouldn't be standing in the middle of his living room thinking about how badly he wanted to run his fingers through her cornsilk hair or kiss her full, perfectly bow-shaped lips. He definitely shouldn't feel exhilarated by the unmistakable desire emitting from her own heated gaze to his, this very minute. Proof that she wanted him, too.

Trust me, baby. I feel it, too.

But in spite of his attraction toward her, Kellan schooled his expression and cleared his throat before asking, "You ready?"

"Yeah." She nodded. "I'm ready."

A few minutes later, he was driving them to her place when he caught himself sneaking glimpses of her here and there, wishing he was staying with her for reasons other than work.

Married. Client. Hands fucking off.

The mental slap reminded him that he was here to do a job. Nothing more, nothing less.

Back at her complex, Mia pulled her keys from her purse to unlock the door. When she went to insert the key, it became obvious the door was already slightly ajar.

Before he could stop her, she pushed it open even more. Mia's gasp was audible when she saw what had been done to her home.

"Oh, my God." Tears instantly filled her eyes as they flew to his.

Sonofabitch!

"Get back." He withdrew his pistol and used his free hand to guide her behind him. "I want you to do exactly what you did last night and stay just inside the door."

Her fingers clutched onto the back of his shirt. "What are you going to do?"

"Make sure whoever did this isn't still here."

"O-okay," she stammered.

Her voice was with her efforts to choke back a sob, driving Kellan's anger toward the person responsible to record heights.

Mia's emotional state didn't bother him. She could fall apart completely, and he wouldn't think any less of her.

But she didn't.

The entire place was destroyed, but when he spared a quick glance at her from over his shoulder, he saw a woman determined to keep her shit together.

That's my girl.

Not wasting time on a mental tug-of-war battle over the possessive thought, Kellan rattled off instructions as he headed down the hall.

"Get on your phone and dial nine-one-one. Tell them you've had a break-in."

The description was mild compared to what had been done to her home.

Mia's couch and oversized chair had both been ripped to shreds. Remnants of dishes lay shattered on the kitchen's tiled floor. Her barstools, dining room chairs, and lamps had all been overturned. Some left in an array of jagged, broken pieces.

And when he got to her bedroom and found it in even worse condition than the rest of the apartment, Kellan wanted nothing more than to shield her from the damage.

"He's gone." He rushed back to her. "Did you call the cops?"

"I, uh..." Mia blinked, swiping away tears and shaking her head.

She pulled out her phone, but her fingers were trembling so badly she could barely dial the three digits.

"It's okay." Kellan put a gentle hand to her shoulder. "I've got it."

With his phone already to his ear, he proceeded to tell the emergency operator what had happened. When he spouted off her address he knew by heart, Mia didn't so much as flinch.

Not a huge surprise since he'd admitted to watching her before.

I'll always be honest with you, sweetheart. Always.

Because something told him she hadn't gotten much of that from the man she'd married.

"He did this." Her voice was wooden as she slowly surveyed the damage. "Elliot did this."

Her eyes lifted to his, the defeat there nearly breaking him.

"You don't know that for sure," he tried to ease her fear.

Yes, you do.

"Yes, I do." Mia parroted his thought. Her watery gaze scanned the destructive scene, her tone filled with utter certainty. "I can feel it in my *gut*, Kellan."

Fuck. He knew better than most how spot-on gut instincts could be.

"The police will dust for prints," he muttered. "It could turn out to be random."

"Oh, come on!" Her raised voice echoed off the apartment walls. "First, he calls me this morning and now this? It was *him*, Kellan," she stated definitively. "It was Elliot."

"I'd listen to the lady, if I were you."

The voice behind them had Mia's breath hitching and Kellan lifting his weapon. With his barrel pointed directly at the man standing in her doorway, Mia instinctively slid partially behind him.

She trusted him to keep her safe, even if she didn't realize it yet.

"Who the fuck are you?" Kellan demanded from their uninvited visitor.

Tall. Dark hair. High cheekbones.

Minus the days-old shiner beneath his left eye, the guy looked like he'd just stepped off the cover of a fucking magazine. And he was staring at Mia as if he'd found his long-lost puppy.

"Easy there, big guy." The stranger put his hands palms up. "I just came by to see Mia."

When he started toward them, Kellan matched the man's forward movement with his own.

"Not another step," he hissed. "I asked you a question." Keeping his weapon trained on the GQ-looking fucker, Kellan bit out a harsh, "Name. Now."

"Shane Devereaux," the man said in a rush. "My name is Shane Devereaux...and I believe that's my sister-in-law you've got hiding behind your back."

"Shane?" Mia peeked around Kellan's shoulder.

Kellan wanted to look at her, to study her reaction to seeing this man. But he refused to take his eyes off the possible threat.

Wait. Did he just say...

"Shane Devereaux?" Kellan narrowed his gaze. "As in Elliot Devereaux's brother?"

"His identical twin brother, to be exact." The man smirked. "That's right. I'm Mia's brother-in-law." That smirk turned into a genuine smile when Shane tilted his head to catch a glimpse of her. "Good to see you again, honey. Oh, and I love what you've done to the place."

"Shane!" Mia slid past him to rush to the other man. "Oh, my God! What are you doing here?"

Kellan had no choice but to stand there and watch as she practically threw herself into Shane's arms. Lowering his weapon, he gritted his teeth, barely resisting the urge to shoot the jerk pulling her close.

Is he really a jerk, though? Afterall, he did help her out of a horrible situation.

Hating that his voice of reason had made a valid point, Kellan stayed back while Mia and her brother-in-law were reunited.

"Hey, honey." The other man let the hug linger a little too long for Kellan's liking. "I came to see you."

"Why?" Mia pulled back. "Is it Elliot? Do you know where he is?"

"I have no idea." He shook his head. "But he *is* the reason I'm here."

Noticing the man's black eye, Mia let her fingertips brush across the bluish-yellow skin. "Oh, Shane."

"Your brother do that?" Kellan asked, doing his best not to imagine a bruise like that marking Mia's perfect skin.

"Sorry." Devereaux's thin lips curled back into a well-practiced smirk. "I don't believe I caught your name."

Because I didn't throw it, dickhead. And you didn't answer my question.

"This is Kellan," Mia rushed to introduce him. "He's my, um...friend."

The description stung way the hell worse than it should have.

Lowering his blue gaze to the gun still secured in Kellan's hand, Shane raised a smartass brow. "Some friend you have there, honey."

She's not your honey, dickhead.

Kellan ground his back molars together before reminding himself that she wasn't his either.

"Kellan's part of a private security team here in Richmond," Mia explained.

"Security?" The other man frowned. "Like a bodyguard?"

"Something like that." Kellan slid his gun into his holster and walked toward them.

With a quick once-over of the mess behind them, the arrogant SOB smarted off with, "Looks like you're doing a bang-up job so far."

"He's trying," Mia jumped to his defense. "His team is

looking for Elliot as we speak. You said you were here about your brother?"

"Yes, Shane. Why are you in town?" Kellan demanded. "Mia told me you two haven't talked since she left Denning two years ago. Seems like a pretty big coincidence, shit like this happening to her right as you show up."

"You think I did this?" The other man sounded genuinely offended. "I just got here. And wait..." To Mia he said, "This guy knows the truth?"

Mia nodded. "Kellan and his team know everything."

A few seconds passed as the apparent good twin let that sink in. "Wait, you said shit's been happening to Mia. What else is there, besides this?" Shane looked to Mia for answers, his worried gaze landing on the bandage near her hairline. "Shit, did my brother do that, too?"

"Too?" It was Kellan's turn to raise one of his brows.

"Well, yeah. I mean, I assume Elliot's responsible for all this." He motioned to the destruction behind them. "Don't you?"

Rather than answer the question, Kellan asked one of his own. "Why would you automatically think your brother's behind this?"

"Because he showed up at my place a week ago claiming I knew where Mia was. He then demanded I give up her location."

"You didn't—"

"Hell no." Shane frowned. "Of course not. You know I'd never betray you like that."

Sadness filled Mia's beautiful face. "That's why he hit you, isn't it? Because you refused to tell him where I was."

Shane's expression softened. "Don't worry, honey. I've had much worse than this. Trust me."

So has she, thanks to your abusive asshole of a brother.

"You said you haven't seen or heard from Elliot in a week?" Kellan verified.

"Uh, yeah." Shane had to practically tear his eyes from Mia before answering. "It's been six, maybe seven days. That's why I risked driving here today." He turned to Mia again. "I needed to see for myself that you were okay."

"She's fine," Kellan didn't give her a chance to respond.

Nice, dickhead. Why don't you just piss on the guy's leg and get it over with?

"Really?" Shane rested his hands on his narrow hips. "Because it seems to me, her home's been destroyed, and she's been hurt. Not exactly what I'd call fine."

"I *am* fine, Shane." Mia jumped back in. "Really. And Kellan's right. I don't know for sure that Elliot's behind any of this. It's just that...over the past week, I've had this feeling that I was being watched. And then my brakes stopped working out of the blue last night, and I wrecked my car. That's how I got this." She pointed to the bandage.

A flash of her car rolling down that embankment—with her inside—struck Kellan hard. But he pushed it aside, knowing he needed to focus on the here and now and not what *could* have happened to the sweet woman with a tragic past.

At the mention of her brakes, however, he made a mental note to ask Greyson to investigate why they suddenly went out. If his suspicions were right—and they usually were—Kellan knew exactly what they'd find.

"We got here a few minutes ago and found her apartment in shambles," he told Shane. "If this *was* Elliot, and you didn't tell your brother where to find Mia, then who did?"

"Got me." Shane gave him a casual shrug. "I didn't tell anyone anything about that night. Especially not my brother." To Mia, he said, "Even when he stormed into my house a few days ago and tried beating my ass, accusing me of everything from helping you to sleeping with you, I still didn't let on that I knew where you were."

Kellan couldn't tell whether the man was being truthful, and that burned his ass.

"He thought we'd *slept* together?" Mia's voice rose an octave. "Where in the world would Elliot get a crazy idea like that? I never cheated on him or anyone else. Not that he could ever say the same." She crossed her arms at her chest. "But even if I had—which I didn't—I sure as hell wouldn't have done it with his own *brother*."

Something flashed behind Shane's blue gaze, but it was gone before Kellan could decipher what it was. He did, however, pick up on the comment she'd made about Elliot cheating.

Not only was the bastard an abusive prick. He'd also been unfaithful.

Remind you of anyone?

"You remember what he's like when he gets in one of his moods," Shane scoffed.

The man's comment about his brother sent a dark cloud over Mia's green gaze.

"Yeah." She absentmindedly rubbed her left forearm. "I remember."

That son of a—

"Ah hell, Mia. I'm sorry." Regret poured off the man as he ran a hand over his freshly shaven jaw. "I didn't mean to bring that shit up." To Kellan, he added, "Look, all I know is Elliot showed up at my place pissed as hell the other night. He was spouting off all kinds of BS about me and Mia and how he knew I was the one who helped her disappear."

The skin between Mia's brows bunched together. "How could he possibly know that?"

"Fuck if I know." Shane shook his head and sighed. "I tried to get him to tell me where he got that information, but Elliot refused to give up his source. We went a few rounds, threw a few punches, and then he stormed off, and I haven't heard from him since."

A moment of silence passed between the three of them before Kellan pointed out the obvious. "If he did somehow figure out you helped Mia leave him to come here, then it's safe to assume he also found her address."

"And my phone number."

"Phone number?" Elliot's brother frowned.

"He called me this morning. On the burner you gave me."

"That bastard," Shane growled. "Mia, I swear I never—"

"I know." She reached up and cupped the other man's face. "I know you'd never put me in that kind of danger."

"I wouldn't." The other man pulled her in for another fucking hug. "I swear to you, I wouldn't."

"Well, he's obviously figured it out somehow." Kellan jumped on board the assumption train and went with the notion that Elliot was, in fact, behind everything that had happened. "So, the next thing we need to do is get Mia someplace safe."

"My thoughts, exactly." Shane seemed to be on his side of things. But then he went and said, "There are two beds in my hotel room. You can stay with me, and—"

"She's staying with me," Kellan announced. "Mia hired my firm to protect her, and that's exactly what I intend to do."

"I'm her *family*." Shane scowled as he rubbed that shit in

Kellan's face. "Mia will be much more comfortable staying with someone she knows."

"She knows me." Kellan held his ground with the arrogant prick. "More importantly, she knows I'm qualified to keep her safe. And if your brother really does suspect you of being involved in her disappearance, he's probably got eyes on you as we speak. Mia stays with you, you'll likely lead Elliot right to her. If you haven't already."

"He's right, Shane," Mia agreed. "I think you should go back to Denning and act like you were never here. For your own safety."

Thank fucking Christ.

"But honey—"

"I appreciate you coming here to warn me about your brother." She licked her lips nervously. "I know what kind of a risk you took in doing that. But Kellan and his team are trained for this sort of thing. There's this one guy, Greyson... He was a Navy SEAL and can pretty much find out anything about, well, anything. If Elliot *is* in Richmond, these guys will find him. I know they will."

When she looked back at him, her gaze was filled with so much trust and hope, Kellan had to fight the urge to pull her into his own arms. Shane, however, didn't seem to want to let it go.

"I'll be the bait," he offered. "I can call Elliot. I'll tell him I know where you are and have him meet me someplace. Once he shows up, Captain America, here, can call his team and swoop in to save the day."

I'll show you Captain America, you asshat.

Mia shook her head. "I can't let you do that, Shane."

"You're not *letting* me do anything." The man rested his hands on her shoulders. "I volunteered."

Yes, and why would a man like you offer up such a selfless act? Especially when, from the sound of things, it would ostracize you from your entire family.

A nagging feeling in Kellan's gut grew stronger as he watched the scene before him. The way Shane's blue eyes always seem to stay on Mia and how the guy couldn't seem to stop *touching* her.

Collectively, it made him wonder if this man wanted to do a hell of a lot more than just protect his sister-in-law.

Could be. Or maybe you're just acting like a jealous asshole when you have no right to be.

Kellan shifted his weight on his feet, the ridiculous thought making him feel antsy. He wasn't the type to get jealous. And even if he was, what did he have to be jealous of? It wasn't like Mia belonged to him.

But you wish she did.

"Please, Shane." Her pleading voice broke through Kellan's thoughts. She rested a palm against her brother-in-law's chest and stared up at him. "You know as well as I do, if Elliot finds out you helped me, he'll kill you. And if something happened to you because of me"—her voice cracked—"I'd never forgive myself."

Kellan opened his mouth to persuade the man to listen to reason when his phone started to ring.

Saved by the bell.

The sound caused Mia to startle and pull her hand from Shane, making Kellan grateful to whoever had chosen that moment to call. Digging his phone from his pocket, he saw Greyson's name on the screen.

With a muttered, "Excuse me," he answered the call. "McBride."

"It's me," Greyson rumbled. "Thought I'd let you know your lady friend is telling the truth."

Kellan slid his gaze to Mia's. He'd already come to that

conclusion, especially given their current situation, but it was nice to know his trust in her claims was solid.

"What did you find?"

"On paper, Elliot Devereaux's a saint," his teammate shared. "But beyond that, not so much. After doing some more digging and calling in a few favors, I found out there are a lot of nasty rumors floating around about the good sheriff. And if the rumor mill is true, the guy's not only an abusive douchebag, he's also up to his badge in bribes, cover-ups, and a whole lot of other shit."

Makes since why a man like that would continue to get reelected.

"Thanks, G. I'll call Winters and—"

"Already done," Greyson let him know. "I called Trace first since he's the one who has the final say and all."

"And?"

"*And...*" The smartass purposely let the word linger. "Based on what I've found so far, he's given Charlie Team the green light to take Mia's case."

Yes!

Kellan released a breath he didn't realize he was holding. "That's great news, but you might want to call him back and let him know someone broke into her apartment while we were gone. Cops are on their way as we speak."

"Shit. Seriously?"

"Yeah. The place is trashed. There's more, but I'll fill you and the others in on the rest later."

He didn't really want to talk about Elliot with the guy's brother standing right in front of him.

"Hate to say it, but that's not entirely surprising."

"Why do you say that?"

"One of the favors I cashed in was from a mechanic who owed me one. I had him run by the impound lot where

Mia's car is currently being stashed, and he confirmed her brake lines had been cut."

Kellan cursed under his breath. "He's sure?"

"Very. He said it looked like someone attempted to make it look like normal wear and tear, but he's worked on cars long enough to recognize a cut when he sees it." Greyson exhaled and then, "Think we need to have another meeting. Get our ducks in a row where Devereaux's concerned."

"I agree. Listen, I need to take care of this situation, and then I'll reach out to Trace to see when he wants to bring everyone back in."

"Sounds good, brother. In the meantime, you find something else you need me to look into, all you have to do is holler."

"Thanks, G. I appreciate it."

"No problem." Greyson rumbled. "I'll catch ya later."

"Later." Ending the call, Kellan slid his phone back into his pocket and returned to the conversation at hand. "That was Greyson." He met Mia's anxious stare. "Trace has agreed to take your case."

"Really?" Her green eyes brightened a little.

"Really." He nodded. He'd fill her in on her brakes later. But first, "You're officially a R.I.S.C. client, which means..." To Shane, Kellan let his smug smirk show as he told the other man, "She comes with me."

Leg hiked. Piss taken. Territory marked.

"Fine." Shane narrowed his gaze just before softening his expression and reaching for Mia's hand. Bringing it to his mouth, he kissed the back of her knuckles and then held it close to his cheek. "If it'll put your mind at ease, I'll go back to Denning and wait to hear from you."

"Thank you." Mia's shoulders fell with relief.

"Anything for you, honey." The man tucked some hair behind her ear. "You know that, right?"

She smiled. "I do."

Kellan stood silent through the whole exchange, but there was an anger bubbling up inside him he couldn't explain. Or maybe he wasn't ready to.

Either way, he *did* want the guy to stop touching her. Like right the fuck now.

Okay, so maybe I'm a little jealous. Sue me.

When Mia finally pulled away from the other man, she returned to Kellan's side. "Goodbye, Shane." Her lips curved into a sad smile. "Go home and stay safe. I'll call you once things calm down."

"Bye, Mia." Shane leaned down and kissed her cheek. "You need anything at all, you call me. Doesn't matter what time."

"I will. And don't worry about me." She slid a quick sideways glance in Kellan's direction. "Kellan and his team will keep me safe."

Turning a hard stare in Kellan's direction, Shane was in full alpha male mode when he said, "You have no idea what my brother is capable of."

You're wrong. I know exactly the kind of man your brother is.

"I'll protect her with my life," he vowed.

"Good." The blue in Devereaux's eyes darkened. "Because if this *is* Elliot, you may have to."

With a wink in Mia's direction, Shane Devereaux said a final goodbye before he turned and walked away.

Sirens blared in the distance as local law enforcement made their way closer Mia's apartment. A few minutes later, the cops were setting up to process the scene.

Over the next half-hour, Kellan and Mia answered their questions and gave their statements. During that time,

Kellan couldn't help but feel a sense of satisfaction in the fact that *he* was the one still with her and not Shane.

She trusts me.

It was an irrefutable fact that warmed Kellan's hardened heart.

He knew from experience, most women in Mia's situation tended to not trust easily. Especially when it came to men.

Knowing she trusted him and his team to not only find her estranged husband but to also keep her safe in the process...that meant something.

For Kellan, it suddenly meant everything.

6

"That bad, huh?"

Blinking, Mia looked up from her plate to find Kellan staring back at her from across his small kitchen table.

"Oh, no," she said in a rush. "The spaghetti's great. I guess I just don't have much of an appetite right now."

She wasn't lying. The dinner Kellan had made for them was good. Better than good, actually. But since she'd spent more time moving the savory pasta around on her plate rather than eating it, his assumption was understandable.

"You've been through a lot these last two days." His deep voice rolled over her.

"I suppose you're right." Mia's fork clinked against the edge of her plate as she set it down. "I just hope your team can find Elliot before he goes after Shane again."

A few seconds of silence passed over them before Kellan asked, "Speaking of Shane, what's the story with you two?"

"There's no story." She shrugged. "Sure, he can be a bit overprotective, but that's because he's like my big brother. And he's a good friend. That's all."

"He's risked a hell of a lot by helping you. Why is that?"

Though his gaze was unreadable, Mia felt the need to be defensive.

"I could ask you the same thing," she shot back. "I mean, at least Shane's family. You and I are...well, we barely know each other. Yet here I am, staying at your apartment and eating your food while you protect me from a man I chose to marry."

And wasn't that the crux of the problem? Everything that had happened to her—before she left North Carolina and after—had been because of the choices *she'd* made.

"You may have agreed to marry him, but you didn't choose to be beaten." Kellan lasered his steely gray eyes onto hers as he wiped his mouth with his napkin and set it down by his plate. "Look, we've been over this, Mia. This is my job. And I'm damn good at what I do."

"So you always bring strange women to your place for safe keeping?" She wondered how many others there've been.

Does it matter?

"Actually, you're the first woman I've ever brought here."

"Really?"

"Really."

Mia frowned. "You've *never* invited a woman to your apartment? Not even for a date?"

"I don't date."

"Ever?"

He took a sip of his ice water and swallowed, his stare never wavering. "Not really."

The admission was shocking to say the least.

Kellan McBride looked like a Greek god, had put himself between her and what he'd perceived to be danger earlier at her apartment, and his homemade marinara sauce was to die for.

The guy had all that going for him, and he didn't date?

She *had* to have missed something. Some sort of red flag that explained how a man like the one staring back at her could be single.

Glancing down at his left hand, Mia said, "I don't see a ring, and there's no tan line from where one used to be. I'm going to go out on a limb and say you're not married."

"Nope."

When he didn't offer up anything more, Mia's curiosity got the better of her. "Okay, so if you're not married and you don't date, then what *do* you do?"

"My job." He didn't so much as flinch. "Which is why I need to know as much about the relationship between you and your brother-in-law as possible. That way there are no surprises down the line."

Aaaand we're back to that.

Made sense, really. Of course, Kellan didn't want her delving into his personal life. To him, she was a job. That's it. Something Mia would do well to remember.

Not like you should be hoping for more. Especially not right now. Maybe never.

A wave of sadness and regret rolled through her because her subconscious was right. There wasn't a man alive who'd want to get caught up in all her crazy-husband drama. And despite having lived under an assumed name for two years, she refused to carry out the charade with someone for the sake of dating.

It's one of the reasons she hadn't become romantically involved with anyone since moving to Richmond. That and the fact that she was still technically married.

And really, up until a couple of days ago, Mia had been perfectly fine living alone. She could do what she wanted, when she wanted, without fear of retribution from anyone.

Sure, spending most of her time locked inside her apartment got a little lonely. Really lonely. But that was still better than terrified, so she'd learned to accept a life of solitude.

Until she'd bumped into Kellan...literally. Mia wasn't sure what it was about the sexy security operative, but the moment they met, something inside her had begun to change.

For the first time in two years, she found herself wanting more. And for a second there, she'd even allowed herself to think that maybe, just maybe, she could find what she'd been missing with the man currently sitting across from her.

I don't really date.

His words were both confusing and sad. A man like him *should* date. Hell, if she were single and someone wasn't trying to kill her, she might even—

"What?"

"What?" Mia was snapped back to the present conversation.

"You looked like you were about to say something."

She did? Crap. She'd gotten lost in her thoughts and couldn't remember what they'd been discussing.

Sensing her struggle, Kellan gave her a verbal nudge. "We were talking about you and Shane..."

"Oh, right. Sorry." She cleared her throat. "Like I said, there's never been anything other than friendship between me and Shane."

"Then help me understand why he's gone to such lengths to help you. Because if his family is as ruthless as you've described, it's hard to believe he'd go against them for someone who, no offense, isn't blood related."

Yes, for someone who didn't know Shane, she supposed it was hard to believe. So, Mia did her best to explain.

"Shane isn't anything like the rest of his family. In fact,

pretty much the only thing he and Elliot have in common is their looks. Elliot's always been power driven, just like his parents."

"And Shane?"

"He's much more laid back."

Kellan mulled that over before asking, "What does he do for a living?"

"Real estate." She huffed out a soft chuckle. "He always used to refer to himself as the black sheep twin, but then he surprised us all by going into the family business while Elliot chose a career in law enforcement."

"Your in-laws didn't approve of Elliot becoming a cop?"

"Not at first." Mia remembered a few heated discussions over the topic. "But after they realized the benefits of having their son become Sheriff, the Devereaux's did a complete one-eighty and became Elliot's biggest supporters."

"What about Shane? Was he supportive, too?"

"Yes." She nodded. "But I think he was just happy he wouldn't have to work alongside Elliot. The two were always being compared. Sports, school, it didn't matter. And Shane resented Elliot for it." Mia blew out another small breath. "The fact that he looked exactly like his brother only made it worse. Before his accident, people mistook him for Elliot all the time."

"Accident?"

"A few years ago, he and some friends went off-roading in their side-by-sides. Shane was trying to show off for the girl he was dating at the time and ended up rolling his Razor down into the creek. He was wearing his harness but slammed his head against the rollbar when he flipped. Split his forehead wide open." She smiled. "I've never seen anyone so happy to get stitches. When I asked him about it,

Shane simply grinned from ear-to-ear and said no one would ever mistake him for Elliot again."

Kellan tipped his head in acknowledgement. "I noticed the scar back at your apartment."

Something told Mia there wasn't much the man *didn't* notice. "It's how the people of Denning came to tell the two brothers apart."

Brow furrowed slightly, Kellan rested his elbows on the table in front of him. "If you don't mind me asking, how'd you end up with Elliot?"

"You mean, instead of Shane?" She smirked. "Trust me, you're not the first person to ask that question. The short answer is, Elliot was a different person back then. Or I guess I should say he hid his true self well."

"Guys like that usually do." Storm clouds darkened the grays in Kellan's eyes.

"Sounds like you're talking from experience."

He held her gaze a second longer before saying, "You still haven't told me why Shane helped you."

I'm expected to be an open book, but his personal life is off-limits. Duly noted.

"Yes, I did." She stared back without blinking. "I just told you, Shane can't stand his brother. And even more than that, he hated the way Elliot treated me."

"And by helping you get out of town, he not only saved you from the abuse, but also gave his brother a giant 'fuck you'."

"Pretty much." Mia nodded.

Giving this some thought, Kellan waited a beat before speaking again. "There's just one more thing that doesn't make sense to me. If Shane hates his family so much, why take a job working for his parents?"

This was an easy question to answer. "Shane loathes the

way his family does business, but he isn't stupid. He lives hard and plays even harder, both of which require a lot of money. So it was a tradeoff. By working for his parents, he gets to keep the lifestyle he wants."

"A lifestyle he risked by helping you."

"Because I *asked* him to." Mia shot up from her chair. Grabbing her plate and fork, she stormed into the kitchen. "He never would've done so had I not called him. So, the risks he's taking? That's all on me."

"Wrong." Kellan walked unhurried into the kitchen behind her. "That was a choice he made. Just like choosing to come here today."

"Elliot will kill him." She set the dirty dishes onto the counter near the sink. The half-eaten pasta blurred as unshed tears welled in Mia's eyes. "He'll kill us both."

"I won't let that happen." He rested a hand on her shoulder and gave her a gentle squeeze. "You're safe with me."

She looked up at him. "I appreciate that, Kellan. I really do. But it's not like I can stay here forever. I'm just so damn tired of hiding, you know?" Mia swiped angrily at some fallen tears. "I haven't always been this person. Before Elliot, I would go out with my friends all the time. We'd talk and laugh, and we'd have *fun*. Then one day, I woke up and realized all my friends were gone, and the things I used to enjoy doing were no longer acceptable. Not for the wife of a Sheriff." She scoffed. "Certainly not for a Devereaux."

Kellan's gaze softened. "If you could do one of those fun things, what would it be?"

The question was moot since she was pretty much on lockdown, but Mia said the first thing that came to mind. "Ice skating."

"Ice skating?"

"I used to love going ice skating in the winter." She smiled. The wistful tone of her voice was obvious, even to her. "There was an indoor rink where we lived when I was little. I remember the first time my mom took me." Mia chuckled. "I spent more time on my ass than my feet, but I loved every second of it. So much so, my parents bought me private lessons for Christmas that same year."

"You any good?" There was a shimmer of light behind his stormy eyes.

"I can hold my own." Her smile faltered. "At least, I used to be able to. It's been so long... I'm not sure I can even *stand* on the ice without falling."

"Oh, I don't know." Kellan's intense gaze bore into hers. "I have a feeling you could do just about anything you put your mind to."

Her chest tightened as she considered his words. "I used to think that was true. Now, I'm not so sure."

"We're going to find him, Mia." Kellan brushed a lock of hair from her eye, careful to avoid her stitches as he tucked it behind her ear. "I'm going to get you your life back."

"Because it's your job?"

"Yes." He swallowed. "And because that's what you deserve."

Reaching up, she wrapped her fingers around his thick wrist as far as they would go. "Thank you."

He leaned slightly forward, his deep voice dropping to a low whisper as he vowed, "I won't let anything happen to you."

Mia rose to her tiptoes, their lips a hairsbreadth from brushing against one another's. "I believe you."

Kellan's gaze fell to her mouth, his desire to kiss her becoming clearer with every beat of her racing heart. Mia tilted her lips toward his, suddenly wanting to feel his touch more than she wanted her next breath.

But then Kellan dropped his hand and jerked away, the move slicing their connection like a sharpened sword.

"I'm sorry." He ran a hand over his mouth. "I shouldn't have—"

"It wasn't just you," she pointed out.

"Doesn't matter." He shook his head. "It wasn't appropriate of me to do that."

"Why? Because I'm a client, or because I'm married?"

"Because you're a client."

Mia licked her suddenly dry lips before asking, "And the other?"

A muscle twitched as he clenched his chiseled jaw, and there was an unmistakable heat filtering through his determined stare. "I would never sleep with a married woman, Mia. But—"

"No, you're right," she cut him off. The rush of disappointment took her off guard, and she had to use every ounce of strength she had not to let it show. "The man may be trying to kill me, but legally, he's still my husband."

"You didn't let me finish." Kellan inched closer. "I've never slept with a married woman, but as far as I'm concerned, your marriage was over the second that bastard laid a hand on you in anger."

"Oh." She swallowed her nerves enough to ask, "And if I wasn't a client?"

"The truth?"

Mia nodded.

With a look of pure, animalistic desire, he said, "Sweetheart, if you weren't a client, I'd have you up on this counter and be buried so deep inside you, you'd be screaming my name."

Holy. Hell.

Mia's entire body became flooded with arousal. Her inner muscles flexed, and her core ached with unprecedented need.

"I-I'm not really a screamer," she stuttered without thinking.

The admission didn't seem to faze Kellan as he rasped, "You would be with me."

He started to reach for her again but changed his mind at the last second. Instead, he took a step back and pulled his phone from his pocket. "I, uh...I should check in with my boss."

"O-okay." *Talk about a sudden change of topic.* Needing to look anywhere but at him, Mia glanced down at their dishes. "I'll clean up the dinner mess, and then—"

"I'll get it." He tapped his screen and put the phone to his ear. "You should get some rest."

And just like that, she was unceremoniously dismissed.

Feeling as though she had a bad case of conversational whiplash, Mia offered him a soft, "Goodnight" and excused herself for the evening.

After a long, hot shower to wash away the last few days, she got dressed in a tank top, panties, and yoga pants they'd bought before coming here.

Staring at herself in Kellan's bathroom mirror, she carefully removed the dressing from her forehead and inspected the damage. As far as stitches went, they didn't look too bad. There were only six, and the cut was so close to her hairline, it was easily hidden.

You've definitely had worse.

And she'd survived them all. With any luck—and with Kellan and his team on her side—she'd survive her husband's wrath this time, too.

7

Three days later...

Mia jolted awake from a restless sleep. Blinking to adjust her tired eyes, she glanced around Kellan's room, noting the sliver of morning light peeking out from behind the curtains.

She let her head settle back into the pillow and sighed.

Every day had been the same since coming here. She and Kellan would make small talk in the mornings, they'd share a meal here and there—usually something he'd fixed.

She'd keep herself busy by using his computer to complete a few graphics jobs while he checked in with his team. They'd eat dinner and then retire for the night. Him on his couch, and her in his bed.

Wash, rinse, repeat.

Every night had been spent tossing and turning, Mia's mind filled with conflicting dreams. Some were of Elliot's terrifying ways. Others were of a different man.

The one whose bed she was still in.

And *those* dreams, well... Those were responsible for the lingering tingles of desire still filling her veins.

She stared at the closed bedroom door and thought about the man on the other side. Or rather, the surprisingly erotic words he'd uttered to her three nights before.

Sweetheart, if you weren't a client, I'd have you up on this counter and be buried so deep inside you, you'd be screaming my name.

A shiver ran down Mia's spine as she lay beneath his covers. She wasn't exactly a sex-on-the-kitchen-counter kind of girl, but for Kellan, she might just be willing to give it a try. Except...

You're a client.

With a frustrated growl, she grabbed the other pillow and put it over her face. Damn him for awakening her long-buried needs when he had no intention of fulfilling them.

He didn't say never.

Removing the pillow from her face, she dropped it onto the mattress beside her. No, Kellan didn't say never, just not while she was his client. Which would no longer be the case once they found Elliot and threw his ass behind bars.

Until then...

Mia tossed the covers from her legs and pushed herself to her feet. Ignoring the room's spicy male scent—that smelled exactly like Kellan—she padded her way to the bathroom. After taking care of business, she washed her hands and gathered her hair into a messy bun, ready for a day just like all the others.

With a deep steely breath, she turned the knob and opened the door. A whiff of freshly cooked bacon and coffee greeted her, putting an appreciative smile on her tired face. But it was nothing compared to the scene she found when she turned the corner and entered the kitchen.

Kellan had his back to her. His charcoal gray t-shirt stretched tightly across his broad shoulders, the material moving in waves with his muscles as he worked the sizzling bacon with a set of metal tongs.

From this view, Mia could appreciate his sculpted male physique.

Strong back. Narrow waist. Taut thighs and a perfectly firm ass, both showcased in a pair of well-worn jeans. And the pièce de résistance...

Brown leather cowboy boots with scrapes and scruffs proving they were more than a simple fashion statement.

Gotta love a man in denim and boots.

"Morning."

The rumbled greeting grabbed her attention, bringing her eyes up to meet his.

Smiling at her from over his shoulder, she didn't miss the subtle way he'd glanced at her thinly covered breasts before asking, "You hungry?"

"Starving." Her lips curved upward.

And getting hungrier by the second.

"Good." He turned back to the stove. "I may have gone a bit overboard."

When he motioned to the counter to his left, she noticed the stack of pancakes, a bowl of scrambled eggs, and a heaping plate of bacon.

"Wow."

"Yeah." He chuckled. "I'm not used to cooking for anyone but myself, and I wasn't sure how hungry you'd be, so..."

"You decided to cook up everything you had?" She walked over to the food with a teasing smirk.

"Something like that."

Picking up a piece of bacon, Mia moaned as the hickory smoked flavor hit her tongue. "This is really good."

"Glad you like it, since we'll probably be eating it for dinner, tonight and breakfast tomorrow." He flashed her a smile that sent her heart kicking against her ribs and a rush of arousal to her core.

"Fine by me." Mia glanced around the immediate area. "Anything I can do to help?"

"If you want to grab some plates and silverware..."

Having assisted with meal prep over the last few days, Mia already knew exactly which cabinet and drawer to go to. Getting them each a plate and a fork, she set them on the counter beside the food. "Anything else?"

"Coffee's fresh if you want a cup. I set a mug out for you." She was rewarded with another panty dropping smile.

Lord have mercy, the man was breathtaking when he smiled.

Clearing her throat—and the inappropriate thought away—Mia tipped her head toward his half-empty mug. "You need a refill?"

"Sure. Thanks."

"It's the least I could do." She grabbed his cup and filled it first. "After all, you've upended your entire life to babysit me."

"I haven't upended anything, Mia. I told you, this is my—"

"Job. Yeah, I know. Still, you took me to get a few clothes and things the other night, you're letting me stay here... It just feels like you're going above and beyond your normal protection duties, and I wanted you to know I appreciate it."

"I'm just glad we met when we did. Otherwise..."

He didn't finish the sentence, but he didn't need to. They

both knew how things would've ended for her had Kellan not come into her life when he did.

I'd either be dead or forced back into a life of fear and pain.

Shaking the unsettling thought away, she held out the mug in front of her. "Here ya go."

"Thanks." He took the steaming cup from her hand, the tips of his fingers brushing against hers in the process.

The contact sent a zip of electricity up her arm and down her spine. From the way he was staring back at her, Kellan felt the strong connection, too.

It was a shame they couldn't act on their mutual attraction. Yet.

"So, what's the plan for today?" She grabbed the plate filled with pancakes and started for the table. "Greyson find any new leads we can follow?"

Talking as he worked, Kellan turned the burners off and grabbed the plate of bacon and bowl of eggs before following her lead. "No new leads yet, but don't worry. There will be. And when there are, *we* won't be following them. My team and I will, while you stay put."

"I want to help." Mia went back to the kitchen to grab her coffee, along with their plates and forks. "I know Elliot better than anyone."

"And I appreciate that." He went for his coffee and then came back and sat at one end of the small table. "But the best thing you can do is to stay out of harm's way so my team and I don't get distracted."

"I understand what you're saying, Kellan. I really do." Dipping out a heaping scoop of eggs, Mia tried to explain. "Look, I don't have a death wish." A fact that should be obvious by the fact that she'd been living in another city under her grandmother's maiden name for the past two years. "But I need to be doing *something* besides sitting around here, waiting for him to make another move. I want my life back, and the only way that's going to happen is if we find Elliot and stop him, and that's not going to happen if we're spending all our time hiding out in your apartment."

"We will find him," Kellan promised as he filled his own plate. "I know it's a lot to ask, and I get how frustrated you must feel. But I need you to trust me."

"I do." As scary as it was, she truly did. "It's hard to explain, but it's like... For the last few years, that man has had full control over my life. Even after I left him to come here. I colored my hair and stopped dressing the way I wanted, for fear of being recognized. I don't go out any more than I have to, and..." She blew out a breath and shook her head. "I know it sounds like I'm whining about nothing, but for the first time in what feels like forever, I finally have a chance to fight back. I guess what I'm trying to say is that I want to be a part of taking Elliot down. I need to be a part of it." After a moment of silence stretched between them, Mia added, "That probably doesn't make any sense to you, but—"

"It makes perfect sense."

The intensity in his stare made her think he meant those words.

"Really?"

He nodded. "He took away your control, and you feel as though you have to be the one to get it back."

"Wow." She blinked. "You really do get it."

"I do." He swallowed hard. "More than you know."

The air around them thickened with the unspoken questions rolling through her mind. But when he broke eye contact to focus on his breakfast, Mia got the feeling this wasn't the time to ask them.

Taking a bite of her eggs, she took a drink of her coffee

before attempting to lighten the tense mood. "What's on the agenda for today?"

With a quick glance at his watch, he surprised her by saying, "We're leaving within the hour, so eat up."

"Leaving?" Mia frowned. "But you said there weren't any new leads."

"There aren't."

Okaaay...

"Then where are we going?"

"You'll see."

She waited for more, but it never came.

"That's it?" She watched him closely. "That's all you're going to give me?"

"Yep." The frustratingly handsome man shoved a heaping bite of pancake into his mouth.

"Seriously? You're not going to give me any more than that?"

"Nope."

Well, dang. "Will you at least tell me what I need to wear?"

Not that she had many options. After leaving her apartment last night, they'd stopped at Walmart for a handful of outfits, underwear, and socks since all hers had been torn to shreds.

"Something warm."

"Something warm," she repeated. "Got it."

She didn't. Not really.

But like he said, she needed to trust him and his team to do their thing. For now, that apparently meant going to an unknown location for an unknown reason, and it was going to be cold.

Fabulous.

When they were finished eating, Kellan had insisted on

cleaning up the mess so she could get herself ready to go. After a super-fast shower, Mia got dressed in crisp new jeans and a hoodie, and put on a little foundation and mascara.

She was finishing up blow drying her hair when he appeared in the doorway.

"You about ready?"

"Yep." She turned the blow dryer off and quickly ran a brush through her hair, deciding at the last minute to leave it down. "Just need to throw on my shoes, and I'll be good to go."

Brushing past him, it was nearly impossible not to react to his enticing scent. Thankfully, Mia managed to keep herself in check.

He'd been very clear about where he stood when they'd nearly kissed the other night, and he'd been keeping his distance from her ever since.

Bottom line, he was her bodyguard, and she was his client. Mia couldn't help but respect him for drawing that line.

The more she was around him, however, the harder it was becoming to control her growing desire for the sexy operative. And as he drove them to…wherever they were going…Mia's mind became filled with the previous night's dreams.

Ones that had starred the man currently sitting behind the wheel.

Focus, Mia. You're not on a romantic getaway with the guy. Find your husband, put him behind bars, and divorce the bastard. Those are your only goals right now.

As usual, the tiny voice was right. The only reason Kellan was with her now was because of Elliot. They could pursue something more personal after this whole thing was over. Until then, she would do her part to keep things between them as professional as possible.

Kellan turned the Jeep into an empty parking lot connected to a large, single-story metal building. Mia scanned the area for a sign, spotting one that read, 'Arctic Adventures'.

"What is this place?"

"You'll see." He chose a parking spot right up front.

Mia shot him an incredulous look. "Seriously? You *still* won't tell me?"

"Patience is a virtue."

"So is knowing what the heck we're doing here."

With a chuckle, he opened his door and climbed out. Grabbing a duffle from the back seat, his tone was playful when he said, "I'm pretty sure that's not how the saying goes."

Sliding out of her seat, Mia shut the passenger door and waited for him by the front bumper. She was about to press him for more when a black Dodge Charger pulled up right beside them.

The windows were tinted, preventing her from seeing who was inside, and at first, Mia was afraid they were about to be ambushed. Seconds later, the car's occupants exited the vehicle, and the breath she'd been holding escaped her lungs in a long exhale.

"Here ya go." The Charlie Team operative she remembered as Asher handed Kellan a set of keys. "I just talked to my uncle, and everything's ready to go. The place is all yours for an hour. All you have to do is lock up when you leave."

"Appreciate it." Kellan took the keys then shook his teammate's hand. "And give my thanks to your uncle."

"You sure you want to do this?" Rhys, who'd been driving the sleek muscle car, stared back at Kellan with the same unreadable stare Mia remembered from when she'd first met him. "If this guy's really watching her, it's probably not smart to have her out in public."

"We won't be in public," Kellan stated with confidence. "It'll just be us inside. As for the outside, that's why you two are here. Thanks for agreeing to do this, by the way."

Sliding a sideways glance in Mia's direction, Rhys brought his cold gaze back to Kellan's. "Just hope you know what you're doing."

"Don't worry about me," Kellan grumbled. "As long as you guys keep an eye on things out here, there shouldn't be any problem."

Chiming back in, Asher slapped Kellan on the back and smiled. "We've got the place covered, Kel. Go on in and let the lady have some fun."

Fun?

With a parting glance in Rhys's direction, Kellan said, "We'll be out within the hour."

Then he shocked the hell out of her by taking her hand in his and leading them both up the sidewalk toward the building's entrance.

Mia glanced up at him. Trying not to read too much into the fact that they were holding hands, she asked, "What was that all about?"

"What, Rhys?" Kellan huffed a breath. "Don't take it personally. The guy's wound a bit too tightly, that's all."

"Feels more like he doesn't trust me."

"He doesn't trust anyone who isn't on the team. Occupational hazard and all that."

When he shot her a wink and a grin, Mia's heart did a funny flip. *Damn.* The man seriously had no idea the effect he had on her libido.

Standing beside him, she waited patiently while he

unlocked the door. Opening it wide, he stepped aside so she could enter first.

It took her a minute to realize where they were, and when she did, Mia had to physically work to catch her breath.

"An ice-skating rink." She spun around to face him. "Kellan, why are we at an ice-skating rink?"

"Why do you think?" He picked up a box that had been waiting for them near the door and held it out to her.

"What's this?" She took it from his hands.

"Open it."

Pulse racing, Mia lifted the lid from the box and gasped. Inside was a pair of brand-new ice skates, their leather as white as freshly fallen snow.

She lifted the skates from the box, doing her damnedest not to start crying like a fool. "I-I don't understand. How did you…"

"When we were talking the other night, you said you missed skating." He shrugged it off as if it was no big deal. "I could tell being locked away in my apartment was starting to wear on you, so I called Asher this morning and asked him to set this up. His uncle owns this place, so he called in a favor."

Mia stared up at him in awe. "No one's ever done anything like this for me. Thank you."

"Don't thank me, yet." He slid his bag from his shoulder and pulled out a set of hockey skates. "It's been a while since I've had these on. You may have to carry my ass off the ice before it's all said and done."

She laughed, the sound almost foreign to her own ears.

A strange expression fell over Kellan's handsome face. "You should do that more often," he murmured.

"What?"

"Laugh."

The uplifted curve of her mouth fell into a sad smile. "I don't even remember the last time I did."

And wasn't that admission about as pathetic as you could get?

"We'll have to see what we can do about that. In the meantime..." He held up his skates and waggled his eyebrows. "You ready to show me your moves?"

With another full chuckle, she teased him by saying, "I'll show you mine, if you show me yours."

So much for professional.

But Kellan didn't seem to mind. If anything, his skin became flushed, and his eyes grew dark with a yearning matching her own.

Flashing her a sexy half-smile, he locked his heated gaze onto hers. For a minute there, she thought he might kiss her.

Instead, he told her, "Last one on the ice buys lunch."

Mia's blades hit the rink a half-second sooner than Kellan's, and for the next hour, he helped her remember what it felt like to be alive.

8

"Looks like you're buying!"

Kellan looked up right as Mia sped past him on the ice as she made her way toward the rink's exit.

Over the last hour, she'd fallen twice. Despite his best efforts, Kellan's ass had hit the ice three times. And he wasn't even mad about it.

He thought Mia was beautiful before, but watching her float across the ice...spinning and laughing as if she didn't have a care in the world...

I'll buy her lunch every day for the rest of our lives if it makes her smile the way she is right now.

A week ago, that line of thinking would've sent him into an instant panic. He'd seen the kind of pain love could cause a person. Back in the day with his parents, and now with Mia and her bastard of a husband.

But the more time he spent with the amazing, resilient woman skating ahead of him, the more he wanted to be with her. And not as her bodyguard, but as a lover.

Too bad she's a client.

True, but she wouldn't be a client forever. And truth be

told, there wasn't technically a hard fast rule against Charlie Team operatives dating clients. Hell, his own team leader fell in love with the woman he'd been assigned to protect, not to mention most of the men who made up R.I.S.C.'s Alpha and Bravo teams.

Kellan, however, had never mixed business with pleasure. Not when he was in the Marines or during his short time with Charlie Team. Of course, he'd also never met anyone who'd tempted him to cross that line.

Only Mia.

The woman affected him in ways he'd never known before. So much so, it was all he could do to keep a safe distance from her these last three days. And nighttime was the worst.

Lying on his couch in the dark, knowing she was asleep a few feet away in his bed... Kellan had to physically force himself not to storm into his bedroom and give in to his primal desires.

But once this case was over—

"Kellan, watch out!"

Mia's panicked voice tore him from his thoughts just in time to realize he was headed straight for her. Her eyes grew as wide as saucers seconds before they collided.

Oh, fuck!

Doing the only thing he could to protect her, Kellan wrapped his arms around her waist and spun his body mid-fall.

Mia let out a tiny squeal as he landed on his back with an *oof*. He could feel her fingers clutching onto him for dear life, and he tightened his hold to keep her body on top of his.

Together, they slid several feet before coming to a stop on the glassy ice.

Cursing under his breath, his first thought was of her. "Are you okay?"

Her head was resting against his chest face-down. She didn't say a word, but he could feel her shoulders as they began to shake.

Kellan's heart sank and his stomach churned. He thought he'd taken the brunt of the fall, but it had happened so fast. Did she hit her head? She already had a concussion from the wreck, and damn it. He never should've brought her here.

"Mia?" He said her name softly. Shards of fear spiked through him when she didn't respond right away. "Sweetheart, talk to me. How bad are you hurt?"

Her shoulders—hell, her entire *body*—shook even harder than before.

Son of a...

"Baby, please." He carefully tried moving some hair from her face. "I need you to tell me where you're hurt. I need to—"

A sudden and loud bark of a sound echoed around him as she lifted her head to look at him. Tears were streaming down her cheeks, but the wide, toothy smile spread across her beautiful face, told him their source wasn't pain at all.

She's laughing.

The crazy, amazing woman wasn't hurt at all. She was fucking *laughing*.

It was the most beautiful sound he'd ever heard.

"You should see..." She tried—and failed—to talk between gasps. "I thought...your face!" She threw her head back as the deep-seated sound grew louder.

"Oh, you think this is funny?" he attempted to scold her, but the smile tugging at his lips surely gave him away.

"Yes!" Mia nodded emphatically. "Oh, my god. That was...I can't..."

She was clearly struggling to breathe for the laughter still rolling through her and fuck it all if it wasn't contagious as hell. Before he knew it, Kellan was lying on the ice with the most beautiful woman he'd ever known in his arms, and he was laughing harder than he had in years.

A minute or two later, they finally regained control of themselves. Both working to control their breathing as they wiped the remnants of moisture from their eyes.

When they were finished, Mia stared down at him with an expression he didn't dare try to name.

"Thank you." She surprised him with a chaste kiss on the cheek.

Using all his strength to keep from reacting to the feel of her lips on his skin, Kellan asked, "For what? Breaking your fall?"

He'd meant it as a joke, since he was the one who'd caused them to fall in the first place, but the greens in her eyes glistened as her expression turned serious.

She shook her head, damn near breaking his heart when she whispered, "For making me laugh again."

"Ah, sweetheart. You should always laugh." Kellan reached up and cupped one side of her face. "Every. Fucking. Day."

Her gaze dropped from his eyes to his mouth. When she rested the palms of her hands on his chest, he knew exactly what she wanted because he wanted it, too. More than he wanted his next breath.

And this time, he was damn sure going to give it to her.

Leaning up, Kellan pressed his mouth to hers. Mia didn't react at first, and for half a second, he thought maybe he'd misread her.

But then he felt her gather the front of his shirt in her fists and pull him closer. Kissed him harder. When her tongue ran along the seam of his lips, Kellan opened his mouth—and his heart—and let her inside.

Even though it was just a kiss, it was the strongest, most intimate connection he'd ever shared with a woman. Because it was *this* woman.

My woman.

Kellan deepened the kiss, his tongue savoring her sweet flavor as it twirled and danced with hers. Flexing his abs, he used his core to pull himself to a sitting position. Ignoring the frigid ice below him, choosing instead to focus solely on the woman in his arms.

Straddling him, Mia moved her hands into his hair. Her fingers raking through the light brown strands as she began grinding her hips slowly against his.

"Mia," Kellan growled.

"I know," she breathed. "I feel it, too."

I bet you do, sweetheart.

There was no way she *didn't* feel it. His dick was so swollen, it ached painfully between his thighs.

If they were back at his apartment, he'd already be inside her. But in a moment of clarity—or maybe it was insanity—Kellan remembered where they were and that their time at the rink was up.

Hating to do it, he regrettably pulled his lips from hers. Kellan was about to suggest they continue this back at his place when a phone began to ring.

Thinking maybe it was Greyson with some good news, he started to reach for his pocket but stopped when Mia shook her head.

"It's mine." She grabbed her phone and frowned,

showing him the screen. "I don't know this number. It's a Richmond prefix."

"Put it on speaker."

Doing as she was told, Mia tapped the screen and answered the call. "H-hello?"

"Mia Devereaux?"

It was a woman's voice. One that, by the look on Mia's face, she didn't recognize. Giving her a nod, Mia understood that he wanted her to respond.

"Yes, this is she."

"Mrs. Devereaux, my name is Kim Bradford. I'm a nurse at VCU Medical Center. I have a patient here who has asked me to contact you."

"Me?" Mia's eyes flew to Kellan's.

"Yes, his name is Shane Devereaux. He says you're his sister-in-law?"

What the fuck?

"Shane's in the hospital?" Mia climbed off him and they both carefully pushed themselves back to their feet. "What happened?"

"Mr. Devereaux was brought into the hospital by ambulance an hour ago with a gunshot wound."

"He was *shot?*" Mia's voice rose two octaves. "Oh, my god! Is he—"

"He's fine, but he was hoping you could come by to see him."

"O-of course." She looked at Kellan, who gave her a confirming nod. "Tell him I'm on my way."

"I will. Mr. Devereaux's in room three forty-two. It's on the third floor of the east wing. Go into that entrance and turn right. The set of elevators there will take you up to his floor."

"Okay. Thank you."

"Have a good day."

Ending the call, Mia looked up at him and said, "We have to go."

She was already pushing her way to the exit before he could even respond.

"Of course, we'll go." Kellan followed her. "Listen, I know you're worried, but you heard what the nurse said. Shane is fine, and if he's asking for you, that means he's awake and alert."

"I know, but...God, Kellan. Someone *shot* him!"

Not someone. Elliot Devereaux.

His gut tightened with dread. This had to be the work of Mia's husband. It was too much of a coincidence not to be him.

And the bastard was escalating. If he'd shoot his own brother, Kellan didn't even want to *think* about what he'd do to Mia.

I'll die before letting him touch her again.

Working fast, they unlaced their skates, replacing them with their shoes. He tossed both sets of skates into his bag before throwing the empty box in the trash on their way out.

Locking the door behind them, Kellan grabbed Mia's hand and rushed to his Jeep.

"So?" Asher saw them approaching and smiled. "How was it?"

"We're going to the hospital. I need you to follow us there."

"What happened?" Rhys frowned, his eyes scanning them for possible injuries.

"Mia just got a call from a nurse at VCU Med Center. Her brother-in-law was shot."

Low curses were uttered by both men and Rhys said, "We'll follow you there."

Waiting for Mia to get buckled, Kellan put the Jeep in reverse. Putting the gas pedal to the floor, his tires squealed as they spun against the smooth pavement. He reached over and took Mia's hand in his.

"He's okay," he reminded her. "He's going to be okay."

She nodded but remained silent as they sped down the road. With her blank stare focused on the passing scenery, Kellan couldn't help but feel disappointed that the memory of their first kiss had been ruined.

A guy she cares about was shot, and you're pissed because you couldn't keep playing kissy face?

His subconscious was right. He needed to quit being such a selfish bastard and be there for the woman he loved.

Whoa. Who said anything about love?

Kellan *liked* Mia. He liked her a lot. But this wasn't love...was it?

"I knew something like this would happen." She continued staring out the window. "I knew it was only a matter of time before Elliot figured out where I was and came after me. I just never thought..." Her voice broke, and a tear slid down her cheek. "I never thought he'd actually try to kill his own brother."

Kellan wanted to tell her it may not have been Elliot, but they would both know that was a lie. The odds that Shane Devereaux had an unknown enemy who'd decided to go after him at the exact same time Mia's husband had started fucking with her were slim to none.

"He didn't kill him."

"Not this time. But I know my husband." She finally turned to look at him. "He won't stop until he kills us both."

Knowing worthless platitudes would do nothing to ease her pain, Kellan chose to drive the rest of the way in silence.

When they arrived at the hospital, they followed the nurse's directions and parked near the east entrance.

With Asher and Rhys watching the area for any sign of Elliot Devereaux, he and Mia took the elevator up to the third floor. The ride was quiet as he wracked his brain for the right words to say. He wanted to come up with *something* that would ease Mia's worry.

In the end, he simply reached over and linked their fingers together, letting her know he was there for her.

"What room did she say he was in?" Mia glanced at the numbers near each door they passed.

"Three forty-two. It should be right up here."

"There!" She pointed to the next door on their left. Pushing it open, Mia rushed inside without bothering to knock.

"Shane!" She went straight to the man's bedside to give him a careful, albeit awkward, hug. "Thank God, you're okay!"

Devereaux was lying beneath a stark white blanket, his left arm secured in a navy blue sling. A large white bandage peeked out from the neckline of his thin hospital gown, and from its location Kellan could tell the bullet had gone into Shane's upper arm, rather than his shoulder as the nurse had described.

"I'm fine, honey." The injured man patted Mia's back with his free hand. "Almost wasn't, but I spun at the last second."

"Was it Elliot?" Mia pulled back. "Did he do this to you?"

Sadness filled Shane's eyes. "Yeah. It was Elliot."

Mia covered her mouth with her hand, her eyes welling with unshed tears. Kellan's chest ached with her struggle to keep it together, and he had to force himself not to physically rub the area covering his breaking heart.

"I'm so sorry. This is all my fault."

Shane shook his head against the crisp pillowcase. "No, it's not."

"Yes, it is," Mia insisted. "He never would've come after you if it wasn't for me."

"Yeah, well...this wouldn't have happened if I'd listened to you and left town like I promised I would."

Finally, something he and Kellan could agree on.

"Why are you still in Richmond?" he asked bluntly. Because the guy *had* promised to leave.

Three fucking days ago.

Shifting his upper body along the noisy mattress, Shane repositioned himself before finally acknowledging Kellan's existence.

"I was going to go back home. After I left Mia's apartment the other night, I went straight to my hotel, checked out, and left. I was halfway out of the city when I turned back around."

"But why?" Mia pulled a plastic chair to the bed and sat down. "We told you it wasn't safe for you here."

"I couldn't leave knowing you were in trouble. Especially since my brother was the one responsible." He grunted as he moved his wounded arm again.

"I told you, Kellan's team—"

"Still hasn't found Elliot." Shane didn't bother hiding his distrust for Charlie Team's abilities. "Not that I expected them to. That's why I stayed. I knew I had a better chance at bringing him out into the open than anyone else. Well, other than you, of course."

Son of a bitch.

"You called him, didn't you?" Kellan stared the man down.

Mia gasped with disbelief. "Shane, no."

"I'm sorry, Mia." He had the good graces to look chagrined. "I thought if I called him and told him I'd give up your location if he met me, I could try to talk some sense into him."

"There is no talking sense into that man. You know that."

"I do." Shane nodded. "But I still had to try."

"Why?"

"Because I want you to be happy, and I know that's never going to happen as long as he's still out there looking for you."

"What was your plan, exactly?" Kellan demanded. "You make the call, have him meet you...and then what?"

Dark eyes filled with annoyance met his. "I just told you. I thought I could talk him into leaving her alone."

"Yeah? How'd that work out for you?"

"Kellan..."

"No, Mia." He shook his head. "I'm sorry. I get that you two are close, but his actions could very well have put you at even more risk. Hell, Elliot may already be underground, which lessons our chance of finding him."

"Shane almost died today."

"Which wouldn't have happened had he just listened to us in the first place."

Mia blinked, her beautiful face twisting with an incredulous expression. "He was trying to *help* me."

"It's okay, honey." Shane chimed in. The bastard's voice was eerily calm when he said, "It's obvious Kellan has grown to care about you, too."

"I do care, which is why I'm doing everything in my power to keep her safe."

"So was I." A muscle in the other man's jaw twitched.

A deafening silence filled the small room as they all took a second to calm down.

When Kellan felt like he could speak without ripping into the smug asshole, he looked at Shane and said, "Walk us through what happened."

"Like I said, I started to leave town, but decided to stick around, just in case. At first, I was only trying to wait Elliot out. See if he'd contact me or show up at Mia's place again."

"You were watching my apartment?"

"I was." Shane nodded. "It's not uncommon for criminals to return to the scene of the crime, so I thought he might go back there to look for you."

"But he didn't."

"No." The other man slid his gaze from Mia to Kellan. "At least, not while I was there."

"So how'd you end up with a bullet in your arm?"

"After three days of waiting with nothing to show for it, I decided to bait him. I called and told him where I was and that I knew where he could find Mia."

A low curse flew from Kellan's mouth.

"What happened after you called him?" Mia asked. "Did he show up at your hotel, or…"

"We met outside of town." Shane's attention moved back to her. "I wasn't sure how Elliot would react, and I didn't want to risk putting anyone else in harm's way. So, I pulled up a map on my phone and found a rural road about five miles out."

"What's the name of the road?" He watched him closely for any signs of deceit.

"It didn't have a name, but I can tell you where it is." Mia's brother-in-law didn't so much as flinch. "There's a stretch of gravel about five hundred feet south of the Fort Harrison National Cemetery. It runs east off of Varina Road and curves around into the middle of nowhere. My brother and I met just past the curve, near the water. My blood's all over the gravel there. I'm sure you and your security guard buddies will have no problem finding it."

The guy's intentionally incorrect description of Kellan's profession had his lips curling.

Don't worry. My team and I will absolutely be checking out that road, you arrogant prick.

With his eyes still locked on Mia, Shane added, "I don't even know how it happened. One minute, we were talking calmly, and the next..." He cleared what Kellan assumed was emotion from his throat. "Elliot seemed fine at first. Or at least he was somewhat calm. I told him everything about that night. How I'd given you the phone months before because I was worried about you, but that, before that night, you'd never once used it. How I got you a new I.D., the car, the apartment...all of it."

"Why go into so much detail?" Kellan asked curtly. "All you had to do was give him an address and then wait for him to leave before calling it in."

"My brother's a cop, Mr. McBride." Shane finally tore his gaze from Mia's to look at him. "He may be an asshole, but he's not stupid. I had to give him something believable, otherwise he would've suspected a setup from the get-go."

"You said he was calm at first." Mia's soft voice chimed in. "What happened to make him so angry he shot you?"

"I don't know. He was okay at first, but then it was like a switch flipped. He started yelling at me for helping you. Went on and on about all the things he'd done for us both over the years, and how we owed him." He huffed out a humorless breath. "He even admitted to cutting your brake lines and trashing your apartment. And then, just as quickly, he became quiet. Eerily quiet. Elliot turned his back on me and started walking to his truck. I thought he was done, you know?" Shane's voice thickened with emotion. "I honestly thought he'd given up and was going to go back home. Next thing I knew, he was facing me again. He aimed his gun straight at my heart and pulled the trigger."

Kellan shoved his hands into his pockets. "Lucky for you, he wasn't a very good shot."

"Elliot's an excellent shot." Shane bit out defensively. "Like I said before, I spun at the last minute. I laid there, pretending to be dead for what felt like forever. He must've bought it because he got in his truck and drove away."

Why are you defending the man who shot you?

Maybe it was the pain meds, but the man's entire demeanor struck Kellan as odd. He couldn't put his finger on it, but something felt...off.

Mia swiped at a new set of fallen tears before asking, "How did you get here?"

"A farmer drove by and found me bleeding on the side of the road."

"You didn't call for help?"

"I would have, but my phone was in my car. I crawled a few feet in that direction but passed out before I could get to it."

"Thank God that farmer found you." Mia reached across the blanket to give Shane's free-hand a squeeze."

"What did the cops say?"

"Nothing much. Not that I expected them to. Like I said, my brother's smart, and at this point, it's my word against his."

"What about the people back home?" Mia frowned. "It's not like the sheriff can just up and vanish without anyone noticing."

"I asked him the same thing. Apparently, as far as his department and everyone else is concerned, Elliot's on vacation." Regret filled the man's eyes. "I'm sorry if I made things worse for you."

"The important thing is that you're going to be okay."

"You're too forgiving, you know that?" Shane brought her hand to his lips.

Mia gave her brother-in-law a watery smile and sighed. "It's my biggest fault."

"Forgiveness isn't a fault," Kellan practically growled.

Her weary eyes met his. "It brought us here, didn't it?"

A male nurse entered the room before Mia could respond.

"Mr. Devereaux," the young man greeted his patient with a smile. "I'm Brent, your nurse for the next seven hours. "How are you feeling?"

"Like I got shot in the arm."

"Shane..." Mia admonished him, but there was no heat in her voice.

"It's okay." Brent chuckled. "A sense of humor is a very good sign." Checking the fluid levels on Shane's I.V., he then said, "I'm going to check your vitals and your dressing. After that, if you feel up to it, I'll go grab you something to eat."

"Sounds good to me."

"We should go." Mia pushed herself to her feet. "Let you get some rest."

"You're leaving?" Shane frowned. "But you just got here."

"It's best if we don't stay here too long," Kellan answered for her. "Now that we have confirmation that Elliot's the one behind all this and that the incidents involving Mia weren't random, I don't want to keep her out in public any longer than necessary."

"You're right." The other man changed his mind. "You two should go. Besides..." He flashed Mia a sideways grin.

"Mom and Dad are on their way. Pretty sure you don't want to have a Devereaux family reunion."

"Uh, no." Mia looked horrified at the very idea. "Not even a little bit." In her next breath, she gave Shane a kind smile as she leaned down and kissed him on the forehead, just beneath his scar. "Get some rest. I'll come by and see you tomorrow."

"I'll be here." He plastered on a less than genuine smile. "But hey, Doc says if I'm good, I'll be able to blow this popsicle stand day after tomorrow."

"Then I guess you'd better be good." Walking toward Kellan, she said, "You ready?"

More than. "Yeah." He reached for her hand. "Let's get you home."

From the corner of his eye, Kellan caught the way Shane's hardened stare became laser focused on their joined hands. But when Mia turned back to give him a final wave, the man's expression changed in the blink of an eye.

Interesting.

Making a mental note to have Greyson take a good, hard look into *Shane* Devereaux's life, he led them to the door. And just in case the man wanted to be more than Mia's brother-in-law, Kellan staked his claim by releasing Mia's hand and put his arm around her shoulder.

Was it a juvenile move? Sure. Did he care? Not one fucking bit. Because one thing had become perfectly clear to Kellan during their little visit.

Married or not. Client or not.

Mia. Was. His.

9

"*No!*"

Mia shot straight up in bed, her terrified scream echoing off Kellan's bedroom walls. Blinking the sleep from her eyes, it took her seconds to remember where she was...and that Elliot wasn't really there.

She was still working to get her heaving breaths under control when Kellan burst through the door with his gun in hand. The muscles in his arm were taut as he held the weapon in front of him, his expression deadly as if he was ready to kill.

"What is it?" He scanned the dark room before looking at her once more. "What happened?"

"Nothing." Mia's lungs fought to return to their normal pace as she swallowed against adrenaline and fear. "It was just a nightmare."

Earlier, when they'd gotten home from the hospital, Mia hadn't felt like being around anyone. Not even Kellan.

So she'd quietly thanked him for taking her skating and to see Shane, and then came in here to shut the rest of the world away. At some point, she must've fallen asleep because the room was dark and Kellan looked like he'd just woken up, too.

Still trembling from head to toe, Mia grabbed the edge of the blankets and pulled them to her chest. Her reaction wasn't fueled by modesty, although the thin tank top left little to the imagination.

No, the move was more about self-preservation. A subconscious act intending to make her feel safe and secure. Of course, she knew better than most that safety was an illusion.

As long as Elliot's still out there looking for me, I'll never be safe.

"Are you okay?" Kellan's deep voice rumbled through the silent air.

Mia nodded but looked away, her skin growing hot from a sudden rush of embarrassment.

Usually when she woke up screaming, she was alone in her own apartment. But since someone had done a serious hatchet job on the place...

"I'm sorry if I woke you." She dropped her chin, focusing intently on the blanket covering her lap. "I haven't had a nightmare like that in over a year. I thought maybe..." Her throat felt thick as she picked at a loose thread. "I thought they were finally behind me."

Standing by the bed, Kellan shoved the weapon into his back waistband. "Everyone has bad dreams, Mia. You don't have to apologize for yours."

"Even you?" Her gaze traveled through the shadows to find his.

Though it was dark, she could still make out the sincerity filtering through his stare. "More than I care to admit."

"If you don't mind me asking, what are yours about?"

"Memories, mostly." His throat worked as he swallowed. "Things I wish I could forget."

"Mine, too." She blinked away tears.

"Want to tell me about them?"

The offer was sweet, but, "Not really. I'm sure you can probably guess."

"That's okay." His lips curved into a small smile. "I never want to talk about mine, either."

When he turned to leave, Mia found herself scooting over and pulling the covers back to make room for him.

"We could talk about something else."

Because I don't feel like being alone.

There was a brief hesitation before Kellan put his gun on the bedside table and sat on the mattress beside her. With his legs outstretched and crossed at the ankle, he adjusted the pillow behind his back and rested against the headboard.

"What do you want to talk about?"

It didn't really matter. Just having him close like this made her feel safe. Still, she should probably say *something*.

"You."

He looked over at her with arched brows. "Me?"

Shadows dipped across his face, but Mia could still make out the man's chiseled features. Even in the dark of night, as he stared back at her, she could see the flames of desire flickering behind his heated gaze.

She nodded.

"Okay." He exhaled slowly. "What do you want to know?"

Everything.

"Tell me something about your childhood."

He stared at her for a beat and shrugged. "Not much to tell, really. I grew up here in Richmond. We had this tiny apartment on the lower west side." His expression hardened slightly just before he skipped to, "I graduated high school and a week later, I joined the Marines. You pretty much know the rest."

"Wow." Mia smirked. "Thank you. I mean, that's so much detail. I feel like I've known you forever now."

Lips she swore she could still taste curved upward. "Didn't realize you were such a smart ass."

"There's a lot you don't know about me."

"Then maybe I should be the one asking the questions."

"Oh, no." Mia shifted to a more comfortable position. "You and your team have spent the last few days digging into my entire life. I think it's time for a little quid pro quo."

"Quid pro quo, huh?" He chuckled. "Okay, fine. Ask me anything."

She thought for a moment and then, "Do you have any siblings?"

"Only child."

"Parents?"

"One dead, one in prison."

"Really?" Mia's chest tightened when he nodded. "Oh, Kellan, I'm so sorry. I didn't mean to—"

"It's all good." He patted her covered leg. "Really."

"If you don't mind me asking…what happened?"

He sat there, staring back at her for so long she realized the question was much too personal.

"You know what?" Mia shook her head. "Never mind. You don't have to talk about it."

"No, it's okay." His brows furrowed a bit. "My mom died when I was a senior in high school."

Oh, Kellan. "Was it cancer?"

"Blunt force trauma to the head."

Mia felt her jaw literally drop open as she stared back at him with what had to be a horrified expression.

"Sorry." One corner of his mouth curled. "Guess I shouldn't just blurt out something like that."

"It's okay." She recovered quickly and squeezed his hand in a comforting way. "Was it some kind of accident?"

"No accident." He cleared his throat. "I don't talk about it much. Or, at all, really. But...my dad used to beat on me and my mom."

Oh, god. "Kellan, I—"

"When I got older and could fight back, he learned to stay away from me. But when I wasn't home to defend my mom, the bastard would take his drunken anger out on her. I used to beg her to leave him, but she always told me she couldn't."

"She was too afraid."

He stared back at her. The experiences they shared so obvious, now. "She always said he'd kill her if she tried."

"So she stayed," Mia finished for him.

"Mom stayed so she could still be around for me, but the bastard killed her, anyway."

Ah, baby.

Mia's heart broke in two. For the little boy who'd lost both his parents...and for the man who was still dealing with the pain.

As sad as that made her to know he'd gone through the same sort of hell she had with Elliot, Mia took comfort in knowing this man truly understood.

"I came home one night to find police everywhere and my dad handcuffed and crying on the kitchen floor." His brows turned inward. "The son of a bitch was sitting in a pool of my mother's blood next to her broken body." Kellan's voice turned thick with emotion, and he cleared his throat before speaking again. "I'd been in the next town over playing in my school's last football game of the season. We lost that night." He huffed out a humorless breath. "I remember all of us on the bus being pissed off and whining about how unfair the refs' calls had been. I had no idea that while I was off fighting for another W on our record my mother was home fighting for her life."

Mia wanted to say something to make his pain go away, but she knew from experience, empty words and platitudes did little to erase years of suffering and loss. So she remained quiet, giving him all the time he needed to let it all out.

"I found out later that, while I was at the game, they'd gotten into a fight. My dad went into my bedroom and got my baseball bat. Cops said that's what he used to kill her."

Unable to keep from it, Mia wrapped her arms around his neck and held him close. "I'm so sorry."

Growing up, she and her parents had never shied away from affection. Once they were gone, she'd been surrounded by a family who saw it as a sign of weakness.

After a while, Mia did everything she could to avoid being touched. By Elliot or anyone else.

But Kellan was different. When he was around, she didn't *want* to keep her distance. Instead, she found herself craving his touch.

Even now, holding this man in her arms... It was like coming up for air after years of nearly drowning.

"I'm sorry," she whispered again. Because really, there wasn't anything else she could say.

Kellan put his arms around her and held her close. They stayed like that for several seconds, Mia relishing in the feel of his strong male warmth and comfort.

Kellan loosened his hold and gently pushed her back enough to see her face. "It's okay."

"No, it's not." She shook her head. "I've gone on and on about all the crap Elliot put me through when what you went through was so much worse."

"We've both survived Hell." He reached up and brushed some hair from her forehead. "And from what I've seen, you've grown stronger because of it."

"So have you." Mia blinked away an onslaught of tears. "God, Kellan. You were just a kid. To grow up in that type of environment is bad enough. But to lose your mother at the hands of your own *father*..." A tear fell from the corner of her eye despite her valiant efforts against it. "That's a level of hell I can't even begin to imagine."

Kellan didn't speak. He simply reached up and thumbed away her tear.

When several more seconds passed, Mia had to ask, "What is it?"

Had she gone too far? Brought up too many horrible memories for him?

Maybe he's regretting his decision to help you.

The thought had Mia searching his gaze for an answer. The one he gave took her by complete surprise.

"You're so fucking beautiful," Kellan rasped.

The unexpected compliment stole the air from her lungs. It also turned her on in ways she never thought possible.

Mia stared back at him, his gaze transforming into a stormy sea of desire she knew had to match her own. The timing couldn't be worse, and though she trusted him with her life, she still wasn't sure she was ready to give him her heart.

As for her body... Well, she hadn't given *that* to anyone

since Elliot. And for the last year and a half of their marriage, she'd done everything in her power to avoid lying in the same bed as him.

But Kellan McBride? Now, he was a whole different kind of story.

One with the most incredible, sculpted body she'd ever seen.

This may be the second biggest mistake of her life—the first was marrying her prick of a husband. But for the first time since she'd said those fateful vows five years ago, Mia decided to take what she wanted, and say to hell with the rest of the world.

No strings. No commitment. They were simply two consenting adults searching for human connection. Something Mia hadn't felt in a very, very long time.

Leaning toward him, she brushed her lips against his and took the leap. "I want you, Kellan."

The heat behind his eyes flared to life. "I want you, too. More than I've ever wanted anyone."

"But?" Because she could sense his unspoken pause.

"We shouldn't do this," Kellan breathed, even as he pulled her bottom lip between his teeth.

"Because I'm married?"

If that was the issue, she'd respect his position and—

Kellan grabbed her hips and pulled her onto his lap. Straddling him like she had earlier on the ice, she could easily make out the way his gaze had darkened with desire.

"As far as I'm concerned, your marriage was over the minute that son of a bitch hurt you," he growled. His Adam's apple bobbed with an audible swallow. "We shouldn't do this because I'm supposed to be protecting you. Not..."

"Fucking me?"

A muscle in his jaw bulged. "You're in danger, Mia. I

shouldn't take advantage of that. I can't... I can't take advantage of *you*."

Smart, sexy, and sweet. The man was seriously damn near perfect.

But Mia didn't need perfect. She needed *real*. And the massive erection pressing against her core was about as real as it got.

"It's been over two years since I've had sex," she admitted boldly. "Even then, it was all about him."

Always.

Sadness clouded Kellan's expression as he cupped one side of her face. "I hate him for what he did to you."

"Me, too," she responded honestly. "But I refuse to give that man any more power over me. This isn't about Elliot. This is about you"—she grabbed his wrist and slid his hand down to her covered breast—"and me. I want you, Kellan. I want to feel your hands on me." Her pleading gaze locked with his. "I want to feel you *inside* me. Please..." Another kiss. "Show me what this is supposed to be like."

Kellan knew he should take his happy ass back into the living room where it belonged. That would be the professional thing to do.

But for once in his life, he wanted to choose what felt good. What felt *right*.

And the woman sitting on his lap...in his *bed*... She felt exactly fucking right.

The physical attraction he felt for her was off the charts, but it wasn't all about that. Especially after today.

Being in a place where she felt comfortable seemed to open her up in a way he hadn't seen before. Seeing her smile and hearing her sweet laugh make Kellan feel as though he was in the presence of a beautiful angel.

And just now, when he'd been lying beside her and telling her about his parents, he swore he'd seen her heart breaking before his very eyes. He'd *felt* the pain and torment filling her veins.

And it was all for him.

No one's ever felt those things for me.

Kellan supposed his mom had in her own way, but she was always so busy trying to appease his piece of shit father to keep him from losing his shit, he'd never really felt the attention and love kids should receive from their mothers.

But when he was with *this* woman...this strong, amazing woman... he felt all that and more.

Mia understood exactly what he'd been through. As much as Kellan hated that, it also gave him a strange sense of peace and acceptance he hadn't felt in, well, forever.

If he wanted her before, it was nothing compared to the need rising inside him, now.

Kellan took Mia's mouth in his. Need erupted and passion grew, and before long, he was kissing her as if his very life depended on it.

Her lips parted and his tongue slid deep inside. Her sweet, rich taste had him moaning shamelessly as held her body flush with his. She was intoxicating to the point where, he wasn't careful, he might just become addicted.

You already are.

Mia raked her fingers into his hair. She licked and laved against his tongue, and Kellan, well...

Kellan. Lost. Control.

In one swift move, he flipped her onto her back and settled himself between her legs. Pressing his lower body against hers, he could feel the heat from her core as it rubbed against his aching cock.

Mia arched her back away from the mattress, her tight nipples thrusting against his bare chest. Lying beneath him, she moved her hips against his, her body searching for the release they both desperately needed.

"Kellan, please."

His dick twitched behind his zipper, its metal teeth digging painfully against his sensitive shaft. It was all he could do not to set himself free and claim the one thing his body craved.

I want her. Only her.

Jesus. He hadn't even gotten inside her yet, and he was already close to falling apart.

Needing to see more of her—*all* of her—Kellan broke their connection long enough to pull her tank top up over her head. Mia raised her arms willingly, her lips curving into a seductive smile that sent his pulse racing and his cock begging for more.

He tossed the shirt somewhere behind him, his focus locked solely on the offering before him. His mouth began to water.

Lying on her back with her hair splayed on the pillow beneath her, Mia was staring up at him with total trust and zero inhibition. Her breasts were bare, their dusty rose nipples pointed and hard, just begging for his touch.

Then Kellan saw them.

He'd missed it at first, his mind too caught up on the fact that they were actually here…doing this. But as he studied her more closely, the sliver of moonlight was enough for him to make out the tiny scars marring her otherwise flawless skin.

They weren't very long, most ranging from a quarter of

an inch to maybe three-fourths. There were at least a dozen of the light marks scattered across her torso. Each one was thin and precise, as if someone had been purposeful in their placement and execution.

"Ah, baby." Kellan felt gut wrenched as he reached for her. Using a feather-soft touch, he traced along one of the longer lines with his fingertip before leaning down and pressing his lips to the slightly puckered flesh. "What did he do to you?"

"When he'd cut me, he always said it was so no other man would want me." Her eyes glistened as she gave him a sad smile. "It's okay if you don't want to—"

He slammed his lips against hers, refusing to give her the chance to finish the ridiculous sentence. Did she honestly think those marks would make him not want her? That he'd turn away in disgust and leave her lying in his bed alone?

Not a chance in hell.

If anything, her scars made him want her even more.

"Those are nothing to be ashamed of, Mia," he whispered against her lips. "Sweetheart, those are proof of just how strong you really are."

"Kellan..." Her voice cracked and a tear rolled down her temple.

Kissing it away, he continued lower until he had filled his mouth with one of her soft breasts. Using the tip of his tongue, Kellan flicked it against her taut nub.

Mia cried out, her fingers digging into his scalp as she arched her back even more in an attempt to get impossibly closer.

"I want you inside me," she panted.

Soon, baby. Very soon.

There was nothing he wanted more than to strip down and drive balls-deep inside her. But she deserved better.

Slow and sensual. *That's* what Mia deserved. And as hard as it was—literally—Kellan was determined to give her all that and more.

Switching to the other breast, he forced himself to take his time. Giving it the same attention as the other, he used his tongue and teeth to savor and tease. Continually reminding himself not to rush.

Show me what it's supposed to be like.

The memory of her recent words was enough to keep him in check. Though his throbbing dick wasn't happy about his slow-down plan, his release would have to wait.

Mia was what mattered tonight. She was the *only* one who mattered.

"Kellan," she rasped his name again. Desperation laced her whispered tone.

"Patience, baby," he crooned. "I've got you."

With the goal of making her forget all about Elliot—and any other asshole from her past—Kellan proceeded to leave a trail of kisses from the center of her chest, down along her toned abs, and below.

Her panted breaths came faster the closer he got to his goal. Reaching the top of her shorts, Kellan pushed himself to his knees, slipping his fingers beneath their elastic waist. Then…he stopped.

"Are you sure this is what you want?" Because he had to know.

"More than anything." There was no hesitation in her answer.

Thinking of the claim she'd made in the kitchen their first night here, Kellan stared deep into her eyes and said, "Then get ready to scream."

He pushed her shorts—and panties—down over her hips and down her legs. Throwing them in the same direction he'd tossed her shirt, Kellan took a moment to commit the vision before him to memory.

Mia naked in his bed. The greens of her heavily lidded eyes dark with desire. Her skin flush from arousal as she stared up at him with wanton need.

When he lowered his gaze, his breath caught in his throat, and his cock wept with need. She was bare and wet, her glistening essence dripping from her needy core.

And it's all for me.

Fighting the urge to release a primal growl of male pride, Kellan gently eased her legs further apart, giving himself plenty of room to work. Her musky scent was intoxicating as he leaned down for that very first taste.

A low, throaty moan worked its way out from the back of his throat. God, she tasted good. So. Very. Good.

Better than Heaven.

Mia's breath hitched, her hips flexing from the feel of his tongue running along her damp slit. For the next several minutes, Kellan took his time, savoring every single drop her body gave him. Licking and tasting to his heart's desire.

It still wasn't enough. But as he continued using his lips and tongue to give her as much pleasure as he possibly could, Kellan realized he was in serious trouble.

Because when it came to this taste...this *woman*...

It'll never be enough.

Mia's body began to tremble beneath his touch, and he could feel her impending release building from deep inside. He was more than ready, too, but Kellan wanted to get her there first.

Working her sex with his mouth, Kellan moved his hand up and slid a finger inside. His moan matched hers as her body clamped down on the digit, the muscles there tight from being neglected far too long.

Soft and wet, he began thrusting his finger in and out of her molten core. Sensing she needed more, he added a second finger, keeping the pace slow and steady at first.

"Oh, god," Mia moaned, her hips lifting upward. Her body's way of searching for the release he'd give his life to bring her.

Following her body's cues, Kellan continued using both his hand and his mouth to create nothing but raw, unadulterated pleasure.

Her inner muscles began to quiver, and he knew she was close. He began pumping his fingers faster. Licked her clit with purpose. And when he put the tiny bundle of nerves between his lips and began to suck, he sent her to the stars.

"Kellan!" she cried out his name.

No, she didn't cry it out. She *screamed*.

He smiled against her most intimate flesh. Her body arched high, her muscles stiffened with her release.

Kellan's fingers became drenched as her inner muscles clamped down around them, and still, he didn't stop.

He pumped harder. Licked faster. Drawing out the pleasure her explosive climax had created.

When he felt her body begin to relax, he pulled his hand free and looked up to take in the beauty that was her.

"That was..." She panted between words. "I've never felt so much..." Her breasts rose and fell with heady breaths. "Wow."

Wow was right. Seeing her in the throes of passion, feeling her body reach a release he'd created...

It was the single most satisfying sexual experience of his life. And it was all for her.

He watched her eyes grow wide as he sucked her

essence from his fingers. "Best thing I've ever tasted," he rumbled truthfully.

"I didn't know it could be like that."

The soft admission was both enraging and fulfilling. It also shattered him, heart and soul.

Not only had the bastard hurt this sweet, amazing woman time and time again, but he'd also robbed her of the pleasure she so very much deserved.

"That's just the beginning," he promised as he pushed himself to his feet and unbuckled his belt before releasing the button on his jeans.

From her place on the mattress, Mia watched him with an appreciative smile and a sated gaze.

"I'm on birth control," she announced. "I get the shot. Elliot never knew, but I couldn't..." Mia paused, licking her lips before completing the thought. "I couldn't bear the thought of bringing a child into a life like that. And after, I stayed on it for fear he might find me and..."

Kellan unzipped his jeans and shoved them down his legs, along with his boxers. Kicking them off, he ignored the painful throbbing in his rock-hard shaft and rushed to cover her body with his.

The need to protect this woman—even from herself—was stronger than any instinct he'd ever had. With that in mind, Kellan put his lips on hers and spent the next several seconds reminding her where she was and who she was with.

When he was finished, he locked his gaze with hers and vowed, "He won't ever touch you again."

Never again, baby. Never. Fucking. Again.

Tears welled in her eyes but didn't fall. Reaching up, she rested her palm against his cheek and said, "Make love to me, Kellan."

He kissed her again. Slowly and with purpose. And when he ended the kiss, he felt compelled to be as honest with her as she'd been with him.

"I haven't been with anyone for almost a year." He swallowed hard. "We're required to get tested for R.I.S.C, and since we just started—"

"It's fine, Kellan." Mia stared up at him. "I trust you."

A satisfying warmth spread throughout his chest. "I'd never do anything to put you at risk. I hope you know that."

"I do." She smiled. "Otherwise, I wouldn't be here."

That was all he needed to know.

"You ready, then?"

"I've been ready." Mia nodded. To prove her point, she let her legs fall open wide and lifted her pelvis to grind her wet sex along his swollen cock.

With a low groan, Kellan reached between them, positioned the tip to her entrance, and took her hands in his. Raising them up above her head, he linked their fingers together. Keeping his eyes on hers as he began pushing himself inside.

He gave a gentle thrust forward. Once. Twice. Inching his body into hers until they finally, blessedly became one.

Kellan closed his eyes and moaned, not afraid to let her know just how good she felt.

"God, Mia," he breathed. "You feel so fucking good."

His words weren't pretty or polished, but he didn't care.

As their bodies moved in synch, he realized being with Mia this way was like being enveloped in pure ecstasy.

It was the perfect combination of torture and grace. A burning fire and soothing warmth. Most of all, making love to Mia felt like being drawn to Heaven by his own personal angel.

As they began the sensual dance that was as old as time, several words rolled through Kellan's mind.

Perfect. Best ever. More.

But there was another word. One he could no longer ignore. A single, coherent thought that continued to rise above all the rest...

Mine.

10

Mia was smiling before she even opened her eyes. At first, she thought maybe it was all a dream. A fantastic, amazing, wonderful dream.

Then she stretched, and her body quickly reminded her that what she and Kellan had shared was very, *very* real.

Memories from the most incredible night she'd ever had flashed through her mind like an exquisite slideshow.

His mouth on hers. His tongue teasing the peaks of her breasts. His lips traveling down to her navel...and below.

Even now, as the morning light snuck past the curtains' edge, Mia could still feel him there.

Kissing her. Licking her. Using his magical fingers to drive her to orgasm.

He'd made her come twice. Once with his hand and mouth, and the other with his impressive cock.

That's never happened to me before.

And the way he felt when he slid inside her... Kellan had filled her to the brim, the feeling painfully pleasurable. Which explained why her body was aching in the most delicious way.

I feel him everywhere.

The memories sent a familiar tingling spreading through her lower belly.

After last night, she would've *thought* those needs would've been more than satisfied. But as the sound of running water caught her attention, and Mia found herself imagining Kellan's hard, sculpted body covered in suds.

She threw off the covers and headed for the bathroom.

It was a bit presumptuous of her to assume he'd want company. After all, he may see last night as a one and done.

If that turned out to be the case, she would handle herself with grace and dignity. Although, the half-opened bathroom door told her that wouldn't be an issue.

Pushing it open wide enough to slip through, Mia didn't have to bother undressing because she'd fallen asleep naked. Wrapped in the warmth and safety of Kellan's arms.

She started to reach for the shower door but stopped. Instead, taking a moment to appreciate his blurred form behind the frosted glass. The man had a body made for sin and a heart of gold.

"You gonna stand there all day and stare or come in here where it's warm?"

A wide grin spread across her face as she opened the door and stepped inside. A cloud of steam billowed around her, and Mia's breath hitched when the water from the second shower head splashed against her cool skin.

"Too hot?" Kellan pulled her body flush with his. The erection pressing into her lower belly proof he wanted more from her, too.

With her palms resting against his chest, she rose onto her tiptoes to place a soft kiss on his wet lips. "It's perfect."

Just like you.

The thought was immediate. It was also a bit unsettling.

The first touch. A first kiss. Those first moments in a relationship—if that's even what this was starting to be—were almost always magical.

It was later, after the newness wore off, when people's true colors began to show. And as she stood under the water, her nude body pressed against his, Mia couldn't help but wonder...

What are Kellan's true colors?

"Stop."

The deep command sent her gaze flying back up to his. "Stop what?"

"Thinking whatever it was that put that look on your face." Kellan reached up to tuck some wet strands behind her ear and sighed. "I'm not him, sweetheart."

Shit. "How did you—"

"Reading people is a vital part of my job."

"I'm sorry. I know you aren't like Elliot." Not even close. "It's just that this connection we have. It's..."

"Scary?" He smirked. "I know. I also know it'll take some time for you to truly believe it, but I swear to you, Mia. I would rather cut off my right arm than hurt you."

He's being sincere. It's up to you to decide whether to believe him or let him go once this is over.

The truth struck her like a giant bolt of lightning.

It was there, in his heated gaze. She could *feel* it in the steady beating of his heart as it thumped against her palm.

It was also in the thought of moving on once this whole thing was over. Of having a life that didn't include the man whose arms were wrapped lovingly around her.

She didn't want to cut him loose. Not once they caught Elliot. Maybe ever.

I believe you.

Though they were right on the edge of her tongue, but rather than offer Kellan the words, Mia decided to show him. Pressing her lips to his smooth chest, she followed the dip separating his six pack until she reached the object of her desire.

"You don't have to—"

"I want to."

Mia wrapped her fingers around his thick girth as far as they would go. Kellan hissed in a breath, his eyes falling closed as she began pumping him up and down slowly.

"Don't start something you can't finish," he teased.

"Oh, I'll finish." She glanced down, getting her first good look at what God blessed him with. "Or I should say, *you* will."

Hard and swollen, he felt like steel wrapped in warm velvet. The tip was already an angry purple, a sign that he liked what she was doing.

Knowing she was bringing that much pleasure to this man was almost as rewarding as the things he'd done to her the night before. Almost.

Licking her lips, Mia couldn't hold back any longer. She wanted to taste him. Savor him. So that's exactly what she did.

Dropping to her knees, she flicked her tongue along the crown. Kellan sucked in another sharp breath, his hand resting on top of her head.

He didn't push her or make any sort of forceful move. Instead, he let her take the lead. With a gentle hold on her hair, he stood still as she wrapped her lips around the tip and sucked him in as far as he could go.

"Jesus, Mia," Kellan breathed.

She smiled as water pelted against her bare back. Ignoring it, Mia began to move her head up and down slowly. Her tongue flicking the tip each time she reached the top.

"Ah, Christ."

His reaction prompted her to move faster. Suck harder. Until eventually, she'd found the perfect rhythm. One that would no doubt send him over the edge.

Salt hit her tastebuds, and Mia nearly smiled knowing he was close. Adding her fist, she squeezed and twisted, her thumb brushing against his sensitive edge as her head bobbed up and down at an even faster pace.

Just when she thought he would explode with pleasure, Mia felt his hands beneath her arms a split second before he pulled her free.

"What are you—"

"Inside you," he growled. "Now."

With his hands moving to her hips, he hoisted her into his arms as if she weighed nothing. Mia wrapped her legs and arms around him, trusting him to not let her fall.

He turned them to her right and pushed her up against the wall. Since the water had been running for some time, the tile there was warm. But even if it had been ice cold, Mia never would have noticed.

She was too busy being stretched and filled as Kellan pushed himself inside her in one long thrust. Mia cried out, her fingertips digging into the skin at the back of his neck while her head fell back against the wall behind her.

Over and over, he thrust his hips against hers. The sound of their wet bodies slapping together mixed with their gasps and moans.

Gone was the Kellan who always seemed to be in control. In his place was a man she'd never seen before. One wild and free as he gave himself over to the pleasure her body was offering.

"Need...you...there," he spoke between thrusts. "Won't...last...much...longer."

Before she could respond, he tightened his grip on one side and slid his other hand between them. His fingers found her clit swollen and ready, and Mia cried out when he began rubbing it in small, tight circles.

"Oh, god!"

He continued rubbing and thrusting. "That's it, baby. Let yourself go."

So close. Almost there. Just need a little...bit...more...

"Kellan!" His name echoed off the shower walls as she came harder than she could ever remember.

Almost simultaneously, she felt Kellan jerk against her. He grunted, his muscles becoming stiff with his own release.

For a moment, they stood like that. Her back against the wall. His body pressing against hers. When their breathing returned to normal and they felt stable enough to move, Kellan carefully lowered her back to her feet.

"Sorry." He frowned.

He's sorry?

Mia's stomach dropped, fearing the 'thanks, but no thanks' speech had arrived.

Determined to keep her composure, Mia pushed back her shoulders and asked, "What are you sorry for?"

"I was too rough." Concern filtered through his gray eyes. "I shouldn't have—"

"Uh, yeah," Mia interrupted. "You definitely should have."

Relieved, he blew out a breath and wiped the water from his face. "You're okay, then?"

Better than. "Yeah." She smiled. "I'm more than okay. In fact"—Mia wrapped her arms around his narrow waist—"I think we need to do that again soon, just to be absolutely sure."

With a deep, chesty laugh, Kellan leaned down and pressed his lips to hers. "I think you might be right."

"But first..." Mia slid out of his arms and grabbed the bottle of shampoo. "If it's still okay, I'd really like to go to the hospital to see Shane before he gets discharged."

"Sure." His lips flattened into a tight smile.

"I know you don't like him, but he's family." Mia began washing her hair. "Well, the closest thing I have to family, anyway."

"Who says I don't like him?"

"Please." She chuckled. "When you're around him, you look like this gigantic pit bull just waiting for an excuse to attack."

"Pit bull, huh?" Kellan squirted some shampoo into his palm. With a shrug, he grinned and said, "I've been called worse."

Laughing, they finished their shower and then got dressed and ready to go. Kellan dressed in his usual jeans, t-shirt, and boots while Mia opted for a pair of black yoga pants, tennis shoes, and a hoodie.

With plans to grab breakfast on the way, they left his apartment and headed for his Jeep. Winter was starting to appear with a few scattered flurries floating and swirling with the light December breeze.

Hand-in-hand, they walked across the lot in front of his apartment building. When they were less than ten yards from his Jeep, Mia realized she'd left her purse behind.

"Crap." Mia stopped walking. "I forgot my purse."

"Okay." He didn't seem irritated in the least when he turned to start walking back the way they came.

But she put a hand up and shook her head. "It's okay." Mia held out her hand for his keys. "I can get it."

"I'd rather we both go."

"Kellan, we just left your apartment, and it's right there." She started walking backward, toward the building. "Just toss me the keys and I'll run up and grab it. But push the fob first to get the engine going so the seats will be warm by the time I get back. It's *freezing* out here."

She could tell it was against his better judgement, but thankfully he didn't spend any more time arguing. It really *was* cold, and the faster she got the keys, the faster she'd be sitting on his Jeep's heated leather seats.

"Fine." He pulled them from his pocket. "But if you're not back in two minutes, I'm coming in after you."

"Two minutes? It'll take me that long just to climb the stairs." Blushing, she added. "My legs are a little sore this morning."

"Just your legs?" He winked and slid his thumb over the button on the fob.

Mia was still laughing when he pushed the button, and the world exploded around her.

11

"What happened?"

Mia looked up from her seat by Kellan's hospital bed to find Rhys storming through the door. Asher, Greyson, and Trace followed closely behind.

"I don't know." She blinked against another onslaught of tears. Her eyes were already red and swollen from crying. "One minute we were standing in the parking lot laughing, and the next, Kellan's Jeep exploded, and he wouldn't wake up."

That was an hour ago, and he *still* hadn't regained consciousness.

"What did the doctors say?" Trace stood with his hands in his pockets.

"Just that he has a concussion." She sniffed. "The explosion threw him off his feet, and he hit his head pretty hard on the asphalt. They said he could be out for a while, yet, depending on the swelling."

Mia couldn't get the images out of her head. The giant ball of fire. Kellan flying through the air. His strong body lying so incredibly still.

I couldn't wake him up. I need him to wake up.

"You seem to be okay." Rhys gave her a once over.

Mia couldn't tell if it was from concern or suspicion. "I forgot my purse in his apartment. I'd already started back toward the building when the bomb went off." Her voice cracked. "It's all my fault."

"Why do you say that?" Greyson asked, his curiosity seemingly genuine.

"He wanted to go with me, but I thought it would save time if I just ran back up myself. But it was cold, so I asked him to start the car before throwing me the keys so it would be warm when I got back down. If he'd come with me, then maybe..."

"If he'd gone with you, he probably would've waited until you were both closer to the vehicle before starting the engine," Asher suggested.

"He's right." Trace's worried gaze found hers. "You could've been hurt, too, or worse...Kellan could be dead instead of just having a concussion."

Mia looked back down at the man whose hand she was holding. A hand that, just hours before, had touched her in ways she'd never known.

Now it was limp and unmoving.

"Where were you guys going when the explosion happened?" Trace asked.

"Here." Mia huffed out a breath. "He was bringing me here so I could see my brother-in-law before he got discharged and left town." She used her free hand to swipe at a tear. "But I haven't left his side."

For a moment, the room was quiet. The only sound that of the monitor keeping a record of Kellan's heartbeat.

Hear that? It's strong and steady. He's going to be all right.

Mia prayed the small voice in her head was right.

Because the alternative wasn't something she was willing to accept.

"We need to find this son of a bitch and soon." Rhys broke the silence.

"I agree, but until we have something to go on…" Trace let his voice trail.

"I can call my buddy who works for Richmond P.D.," Greyson offered. "He's part of the Major Crimes Division. I bet he could round up a female officer who could pass for Mia."

Asher rested his hands on his hips. "You talking about baiting Devereaux into a meet?"

"We gotta do something." Greyson shrugged one of his big shoulders. "We know the guy has a hard-on for Mia, but now he's targeted Kellan."

"You think the bomb was meant to take him out?" Asher frowned.

"Makes sense." Trace chimed in. "Kellan was there when her brakes went out. He was there when they discovered the mess at her apartment. Elliot could've planted the bomb hoping to get Kellan out of the way so he could get to Mia."

Oh, god.

As the men continued brainstorming ways to bring Elliot out in the open, Mia thought about what could've happened had Kellan been just a few feet closer to the bomb.

He could've died.

Mia drew in a shaky breath as she accepted the awful, ugly truth. Kellan could've died today, and it would've been her fault.

"I think you're right." Trace's deep voice tore Mia away from her thoughts. "The only way we're going to have a chance at nabbing this guy is if he thinks there's a chance he can get to Mia." To Greyson he started to say, "Call your friend at Major Crimes. See if he can find a—"

"No." Mia shook her head.

All four men turned in her direction, but it was Rhys—of course—who responded first.

"What do you mean, no? Do you not see what's happening here? You went to Kellan for help because you felt like your husband had found you. Well, guess what? He did, and Kellan damn near died today because he was protecting you."

"Maddox..." Asher warned.

But Rhys didn't want to hear it. "No, Asher," the guy snapped. "She claims to want our help, but now that we actually have a plan that might work, she's saying no."

"I'm not saying no to the plan." Mia regrettably released Kellan's hand and set it gently onto the mattress beside his blanketed leg. Standing, she kept her shoulders back and her chin jutted as she faced off with the dark-haired operative. "I'm saying using another woman in my place won't work."

"Why not?" Rhys challenged.

But this was one fight she was determined to win. "Because Elliot is a lot of things, but dumb isn't one of them. It's the reason he's gotten away with so much for so long."

"Fine." Rhys crossed his muscled arms at his chest. "You think you can come up with a better idea, be my guest."

I've got the best idea of all.

"You want to set up a meet, that's fine. But I need to be the one who goes, not some undercover cop he'll spot a mile away."

The room erupted in low voices talking all at once. Most were conveying their disapproval of her idea.

"Mia, that's mighty brave of you, but we can't let you do that."

She stared up into Greyson's golden eyes. "I appreciate that, Greyson, but it's not your decision."

"No, G's right." Asher piped up again. "Kellan will have our asses if he wakes up to find out we stood back while you walked into the lion's den."

"And how do you think he'll feel knowing we let Elliot get away with damn near killing him?"

These guys just didn't get it. She understood why they were being protective. After all, that's the whole reason she hired them.

But for the first time in years, Mia felt she had a reason not to simply exist, but to *live*. And that man was lying in a bed a foot away, injured and unconscious because her psycho of a husband couldn't seem to let her go.

This was her mess. She'd made it five years ago when she married a monster. It was long past time she cleaned it up.

"He's not getting away with anything," Trace promised. "We're going to find him. But we can't put you in harm's way to do it."

As the men continued to discuss their plan as if she wasn't there, Mia looked over at Kellan, who was still out cold. Fresh scratches and scrapes were etched across his cheeks and chin, and her heart broke more and more with every second he lay there.

No more.

Decision made, she pulled out her phone to dial the number she thought she'd never call again. Her nerves were shot, but she pushed all that away. She had to do this.

For Kellan.

For me.

Mia tapped her screen to start the call and put her phone to her ear. Elliot answered on the second ring.

"Well, hello, sweet wife." His voice sent a chill down her spine. "Finally come to your senses, have you?"

You have no idea.

"You win," Mia said firmly.

The group of men stopped talking and turned to her, but she ignored them and focused on the man she despised more than anything in the entire world.

"I usually do win," Elliot mused. "Something you should know by now."

"I'll come back to you on one condition."

Trace and the others—including Rhys—began shaking their heads vehemently. Greyson motioned toward the phone and mouthed for her to put it on speaker.

Pulling the phone away from her ear, Mia tapped the screen again so they could hear both sides of the conversation.

"You're giving me a condition?" Elliot chuckled in that arrogant way of his. "This should be good."

With her gaze locked on Rhys's, she said, "I'll come back to you willingly if you promise me no one else will get hurt."

"I don't know if you're referring to my brother or your boyfriend. Either way, that was all your fault. None of this would've happened if you'd stayed home, where you belong, instead of running away in the middle of the night like a fucking coward. You forced my hand, Mia. I didn't want to hurt anyone. Just remember that. *You* caused this. Not me."

"I know." Mia bit her tongue to keep from ripping into him. "I'm...sorry."

"Not as sorry as you're going to be."

The ominous words had the men in the room turning to

stone. Even Rhys looked like he wanted to kill Elliot for threatening her the way he had.

"But that's all right," Elliot continued. "We all make mistakes. The important thing is that you recognize the error of your ways, and you're willing to admit you were wrong to leave me."

I wasn't wrong, you self-righteous son of a...

"Where do you want to meet?" Mia was proud of herself for keeping a soft, steady voice. "Give me a place and a time, and I'll be there."

There was a moment of silence before Elliot said, "How about the place where I shot my brother? I'm sure he's told you all about it by now."

"He did." Mia felt nauseated at how flippant the man could be when discussing shooting his own flesh and blood. "So you want me to come to the same gravel road? The one off of Varina?"

"Just past Fort Harrison National Cemetery." Elliot sounded as if he were impressed that she could remember the name of a road. "That's right."

The man always did underestimate her. Today, he was going to find out just how big a mistake that is.

"When do you want me there?"

Another pause and then, "Two hours?"

Her pulse raced with fear and anticipation. "I'll be there."

"Don't be late, my love. You know how much I hate to be kept waiting."

"I remember." She swallowed the memories away. "I'll see you in two hours."

"I can hardly wait."

Ending the call, Mia bent over at the waist and rested her hands on her knees. Feeling as though she were about to throw up, she forced herself to take several slow, deep breaths.

"What the hell were you thinking?" Rhys demanded.

Mia drew in one final breath before standing upright and facing the firing squad. "I was thinking that I'm tired of seeing the people I love get hurt because they were trying to protect me."

Asher's dark brows rose high. He glanced around at the others before bringing his gaze back to hers. "Did you just say you love Kellan?"

"No." Mia thought back over her words, and...crap. "Maybe. Look, that's not what's important right now. The point is, I have a chance to end this whole thing today. Now you guys can be mad at me if you want, but I *will* be on that road in two hours. With or without your help."

The corner of Greyson's lips twitched, as did Trace's. Rhys's expression was unreadable, but Asher didn't even bother trying to hide his growing smile.

"If Kellan doesn't marry you, I sure as hell will."

Mia couldn't help but give the young operative a small smile of her own. One that faltered with Trace's next words.

"You realize Elliot could be planning to kill you the second he sees you."

Yes. She'd be a fool not to come to that conclusion. Still, "That's a risk I'm willing to take."

"There are other options," Trace continued. "You could leave town. Start over someplace else. We have the connections to help you disappear."

"So I can spend the rest of my life waiting for something like this to happen again?" Mia shook her head. "I appreciate the offer, Trace, but no." Looking around at the others, she said, "Look, I get that this is dangerous. Possibly suicidal. But I'd rather die than go back to that man, and I know deep in my gut that this is my only shot at stopping Elliot for good."

"And if you die in the process?" Asher posed the question quietly. "Think about what that would do to Kellan."

"I am thinking about Kellan." She took a second to gather her courage before telling him, "You were right before. I do love him. I don't know how it happened so quickly, or how he feels about me. Hell, I don't even know if there's any kind of future there. But as long as my husband is walking around a free man, we'll never get the chance to find out." When the men remained quiet, she added, "My safety aside, that man almost killed one of your teammates. I know you want to catch him as badly as I do. I also know that *I'm* the best shot you have of making that happen."

A full minute passed before anyone said a word. When they did, it was Rhys who spoke up first.

"She's right." His change in attitude was surprising. "We're no closer to catching this son of a bitch than we were five days ago. She's already set up the meet with Devereaux, so I say we see it through.

Greyson nodded. "I'll call my friend with the RPD. See if he can put a team of officers together to meet us out there."

"You want to bring the locals in on this?" Asher frowned. "That doesn't sound like you."

"I'm willing to do whatever it takes if it means keeping Kellan's woman safe." Greyson glanced at his teammates as if he was waiting for one of them to argue.

Thankfully, none of them did.

"Pull up an ariel view of the area so we can see what we have to work with." Trace motioned toward the tablet in Greyson's hand.

Something told Mia the thing was never very far from his reach.

Everyone waited while the former SEAL did his thing. Fortunately, they didn't have to wait long.

"That section of property is lined with trees," he shared. "So there's plenty of places for us and local authorities to set up without being seen."

"So what exactly is the plan?" Asher asked no one in particular. "We wait for Devereaux to show and then take him down?"

"Sounds simple enough to me." Trace nodded. He turned to Mia. "You sure about this?"

Mia gave the man a solemn nod.

After studying her for another beat, the man in charge turned to Greyson and said, "Make the call."

While the men did their thing to get ready, Mia sat back down and took Kellan's hand in hers. Lifting it to her lips, she kissed the back of his knuckles before turning her head and resting her cheek there.

Silently in her mind, she told him all the things she needed to before walking into battle.

I'm sorry, Kellan. I know you're going to be mad, but I hope you'll find it in your heart to forgive me. Because I don't know about you, but I really want to try to make this thing with us work. And that can't happen until I put an end to this for good. Oh, and one more thing...I love you. It's crazy and fast, but it's the truth. I promise I'll tell you for real once you wake back up. So rest now. I promise I'll be back soon.

Mia laid Kellan's hand back down onto the mattress. Standing, she leaned over the metal railing and placed a lingering kiss on his forehead before turning and facing his team.

"Okay." She blew out a breath. "Tell me what I need to do."

12

"She did *what*?"

Kellan stared at Asher as if he'd lost his damn mind. There was a ringing in his ear, after all. Nasty little side effect from nearly being blown to bits.

He'd woken up a few minutes ago with a pounding headache and Mia's name on his lips. He'd opened his eyes, hoping to see her beautiful, smiling face.

Instead, he found Asher. His teammate and friend who, after enduring several minutes of Kellan threatening to beat his ass, finally copped to where Mia really was.

"Relax. Things have been radio silent on this end, which means she's fine. You'd know if something went sideways. Trace would've—"

A humorless laugh bubbled up from deep inside as Kellan threw off his covers and started to stand. "I must've hit my head a hell of a lot harder than I thought, because there's no way I heard that shit right."

With his IV hand on the metal pole beside him, he let his bare feet slap against the cold tile floor a fraction of a second before his ass damn near did. With a muttered curse,

Asher shot up from his chair and hooked his arm around Kellan's to keep him from falling.

Fuck me. Kellan closed his eyes and put his head in his hands.

"Take it easy, man." Asher guided him and the pole back to the bed. "You have a pretty bad concussion going on in there."

That would explain the sledgehammers smashing against my skull.

"I wake up from almost getting my ass blown all to hell, only to find out that the woman I"—he cut the declaration short. Taking a deep, cleansing breath, he restated it by saying, "I wake up to find out Mia's out there right now, acting as bait for the asshole who's made her life a living hell, and you want me to take it *easy?*" His glare shot daggers at the other man. "I can't believe you guys actually agreed to let her do this. What the *fuck* were you thinking?"

"Look, I know you're upset," Asher muttered the massive understatement. "But we've got her covered. Trace, Rhys, and Greyson are all there, plus Grey called in a detective friend of his and got Richmond P.D.s Major Crimes unit in on it."

"Great." Kellan huffed. "So they'll all have a front-row view if Devereaux decides to shoot her the same way he shot his own fucking brother!" He stood again, taking things a bit slower this time. Once he was sure he wouldn't faceplant at his teammate's feet, he began looking around the room as he demanded, "Get me my clothes."

"The uh...the staff cut them off when you were first brought in."

Fanfuckingtastic.

"Fine," he barked. "Then get me some scrubs."

"Seriously, man." Asher continued to try to calm him

down. "You've been unconscious for a while. You can't just walk out of here the minute you wake up."

"The fuck I can't." Kellan growled. With his bare ass hanging out, he began opening and closing the room's cabinets. "And where are my shoes?"

Rather than help with his search, Asher kept his voice steady and sighed. "Kellan, Mia was supposed to meet up with Devereaux over an hour ago. The guy's probably being put into cuffs as we speak."

Ignoring his teammate's logic, he said, "Either find me some goddamn clothes, or I'm leaving in this. Either way, you're going to take me to Mia right the fuck now!"

"I'm right here."

The soft voice he'd been craving to hear from the minute he woke up had both men turning to see Mia standing in the open doorway. The rest of his team were gathered in the hallway behind her.

Thank God.

Ignoring the wave of dizziness rolling through his brain and the tube running from the back of his hand, Kellan wheeled his I.V. stand to where she was standing and pulled her into his arms. "Are you okay?" He gave himself a moment to let go of the fear coursing through him. "He didn't hurt you, did he?"

Not waiting for a response, he took a step back and began scanning her for injuries.

"I'm fine." She grabbed his free hand and squeezed. "Elliot never even showed."

"What?" Asher didn't bother hiding his surprise.

Their words barely registered through the red haze of anger Kellan still felt toward his team.

"I can't believe you'd put her in danger like that." The hissed words were directed at his team leader.

"I was never in any danger, Kellan," Mia assured him.

"She's right." Trace held up a hand in an attempt to ease the tension in the room. "Devereaux was a no-show."

"It doesn't make sense." Mia shook her head. "As far as Elliot knew, I was giving him what he wanted."

Kellan could barely stomach the thought.

"Think someone tipped him off?" Asher asked no one in particular.

"Who?" Rhys chimed in. "No one but us and local P.D. knew about the meet."

"Maybe that's it." Mia's emerald gaze traveled around the group. "Elliot has connections with several law enforcement agencies. Maybe someone inside Richmond P.D. gave him a heads up."

"If they did"—Greyson's deep voice rumbled—"my friend will find out. And don't worry, Luke's one of the good guys."

Feeling as though he was about to implode, Kellan looked to his teammates and said, "Can you guys give us a minute?"

With a few understanding nods, the others turned around and left the room. Mia started talking the second the door snicked close.

"Don't be mad at them," she spoke softly. "This was all my idea. They didn't even want to go through with it. I had to fight to talk them into it."

"Why?" He flexed his fist at his side. When he thought about what could've happened to her...

"I had to."

"No, you didn't."

"Yes, I did." Mia walked toward him, her voice lowering to almost a whisper. "He almost killed you today. If you hadn't stopped walking across that parking lot when you did, you'd be dead right now." A tear escaped the corner of her eye, but she wiped it dry and went on. "I've been scared before, Kellan. I thought...I thought the day Elliot put that gun to my head was the absolute worst moment of my life. But then I saw you lying on the ground. You were hurt and so still." Her voice cracked. "I tried to wake you up, but you wouldn't open your eyes, and I knew then that there was something even more terrifying than having to face Elliot again."

"What?" Kellan had to ask.

Her watery gaze remained on his as she said, "Losing you."

Ah, baby. "Mia, I—"

"I've spent so much of my life being afraid." She moved closer. She didn't stop until there were mere inches separating them. "To live. To love." Mia placed a palm to his chest. "I know I'm risking a lot by telling you this. It's crazy and fast...I mean, we've only known each other what, a week? Hell, this may send you running for the hills, but even if it does, at least I'll know I was being honest. With you...with myself. Because I'm done being afraid."

"What is it, sweetheart?" Kellan cupped her cheek with his free hand. "You can tell me anything."

She licked her lips, her hesitation lasting only a second. "Kellan, I—"

"I heard you were awake." A nurse chose that moment to walk into the room. "Glad to see you're feeling up to moving around, Mr. McBride, but we need to get you back in bed so I can check your vitals."

Worst timing ever, lady.

The friendly African American woman gave him no choice when she pulled the I.V. stand from his hand and practically pushed him back toward the bed.

Kellan allowed it to happen, but only because he didn't want to make a complete ass out of himself in front of Mia.

"How are you feeling?"

Like my head's about to explode right off my shoulders. "I'm fine."

"Mmm hmm." The middle-aged woman didn't hide her disbelief. "Any dizziness or blurred vision?"

"A little," he answered honestly. "Nothing I can't handle."

"That's great." She smiled. "I'm just going to see how your lungs and blood pressure's doing, and then the doctor will be in to check on you."

"I'm going to go use the restroom while you guys do your thing," Mia announced. "I'll be right back."

He started to tell her to wait, but she was already gone. Like the good patient he was, Kellan followed the nurse's instructions, taking several deep breaths while she pressed her cold stethoscope against his back.

He half-listened as she talked, his mind still stuck on the conversation he and Mia were having just before they were interrupted.

Kellan thought he knew was she was about to confess, but something like that was too important for him to assume. The second she got back from the bathroom, however, they were going to finish their little talk. Because he had to know...

Does she love me, too?

MIA TURNED ON THE FAUCET AND FILLED HER PALM WITH A few pumps of foamy soap. As she washed her hands, she began to re-think her decision to tell Kellan how she really felt about him.

Was it too soon to be in love? Most people would answer that question with a resounding yes. But Mia knew the love she felt for Kellan was real. As real as the heart beating wildly inside her chest.

She wondered how he'd react when she actually said the words out loud. Would he put on a brave face and placate her with empty promises he thought she'd want to hear?

No, not Kellan. If there was anything she'd learned over the last several days, it was that he was a man of his word.

Whatever his response, whether he shared her same feelings or he didn't, Mia knew it would be honest and truthful. And as she looked at her weary reflection, she realized that's all she really wanted.

Memories from that morning flashed before her. Them in the shower. Kellan grunting her name as he came.

Okay, so maybe I want more. A whole lot more.

Smiling at the prospect, Mia was just finishing rinsing her hands when a woman came out of the stall behind her. Their eyes met, and for a minute, she couldn't breathe.

"Well, well, well." Catherine Devereaux—Elliot and Shane's mother—gave her a snarky grin. "If it isn't the little troublemaker, herself."

The last three years hadn't been kind to the tall, slender woman. Her blonde hair had turned almost entirely silver, and there were several new wrinkles trying to peak through behind the Botox injections she'd gotten in an effort to hide them.

As always, Catherine was dressed to the nines with a patterned red wrap-around dress that stopped mid-calf, red heels, and shiny jewelry that probably cost a small fortune.

In the past, Mia would've cowered down and taken the

verbal beating without retort. But things had changed. *She'd* changed. And she refused to be anyone's punching bag—physical or otherwise—ever again.

"I'm not the troublemaker, Catherine." Mia yanked loose three paper towels from the holder mounted on the wall. "That would be your son."

"Elliot did nothing but provide for you, and what did you do to him in return? You *humiliated* him in front of the entire town. The county even." Her voice rose with dramatics. "Sneaking off like some sort of thief in the night. That was low, even for someone like you."

"Someone like me?" Mia turned and faced her. For the first time in her life, she didn't feel intimidated by the aging woman, and damn if it didn't feel good.

"Yes, dear. Someone like you. A middle-class girl whose parents barely made ends meet. It's no wonder you weaseled your way into Elliot's life the way you did. Not that I can blame you. After all, money and stature can be a very attractive quality when searching for a man to rescue you from near poverty."

God, she really is a grade-A bitch.

"Let's get a few things straight, shall we?" Mia stepped closer to the vile woman. "Your son is an abusive son of a bitch who doesn't care about anyone or anything, other than himself. Do you even know the number of times he hit me? I lost count after twenty-three. He gave me countless black eyes, cracked several ribs, and broke my arm in two places by throwing me down the front steps of our home. That last one happened the night I 'snuck away'. You want to know what finally gave me the strength to leave? It was the moment he put a gun to the back of my head and threatened to kill me."

"Elliot would never—"

"He *admitted* it all to Shane!" Mia's raised voice echoed off the bathroom walls. "How he cut the brake lines on my car so I would wreck. Trashing my apartment. All of it. But you probably already knew about it, too, didn't you? You, your husband...hell, the whole damn town knows what kind of man your son is. They just never had the guts to stand up to him...or to you. Neither did I, until now. But you don't scare me, anymore, Catherine. Neither does Elliot."

"If you think you can stand here and slander my family's good name with your delusional lies, you're an even bigger fool than I thought."

"Everything I said was the truth, and you damn well know it. Oh, and just a heads up...the entire Richmond Police Department is out there looking for Elliot as we speak. They *will* find him, and when they do, everyone will know the truth. About him, you, and your fucked up family."

"At least I still have a family," she shot back. "Without Elliot, you have nothing. You *are* nothing. And you'll always be nothing."

Though she wanted to punch the hateful woman in the throat, Mia kept her composure as she smiled and said, "Better than being a Devereaux."

Huffing out a hoity toity breath, Catherine stormed toward the door as if to leave. But Mia had one final thing she needed to say.

"Oh, and Catherine?" She waited until Elliot's mother faced her to continue. "If you ever speak about my parents like that again, I'll—"

"You'll what?"

Looking the square in her cold blue eyes, Mia vowed, "I'll fucking kill you."

With a dramatic gasp, Catherine Devereaux spun on her

designer heels and stormed out of the room, leaving Mia alone to deal with her racing heart.

The sound of a toilet flushing startled her, and she turned to see a face she knew but couldn't quite place.

"Damn, girl." The tiny blonde gave her an approving nod. "Remind me never to get on your bad side."

"I'm sorry." Mia cringed. "I didn't realize anyone else was in here."

"Are you kidding?" She began washing her hands. "That was the best thing I've heard in...I don't know how long."

"I'm not usually a confrontational person." And by not usually, she meant *never*. "I don't know what came over me." Mia studied her closely. "I'm sorry. I know we've met, but I can't quite seem to place you."

"I'm Emma Cooper." The adorable woman held out her hand. "I manage the office for Charlie Team, and I'm Trace's fiancée."

"That's right." Mia shook her hand. "We met the other day when Kellan and I came to the office."

"That was me." Her smile grew wide a second before it fell. "Hey, I'm sorry about everything that's happened. Trace called me right after the explosion, but I was on a conference call with a potential client, or I would've been here sooner. How's Kellan doing? Trace said he's finally awake?"

"Yeah." Mia nodded. "A little grumpy, but he's okay." *Thank God.*

"That's great. And hey, don't ever feel the need to apologize for standing up for yourself."

"I just wish I'd done it sooner." She sighed. If I had, Kellan wouldn't be lying in that damn hospital bed."

The two women exited the restroom.

"Regret can be a fickle bitch, that's for sure," Emma

commented. "Of course, sometimes the very best things in life can come from the absolute worst situations."

Something in her tone had Mia asking, "Are you speaking from experience?"

"Maybe." She grinned. "Hey, you want to go grab a cup of coffee? I spotted a little shop down at the end of the hall when I first got here."

Caffeine sounded like a godsend right about now. But...

"I don't know." Mia glanced down to where the team was still standing around outside Kellan's door. "I should probably get back."

"There's trouble." Asher joined them after leaving the men's restroom next door. "You two look like you're conspiring against the world. Should I be worried?"

Emma chuckled. "Hey, Ash. Not the world. Just some much needed caffeine."

"You going to the shop down the hall?" He looked in Mia's direction. "If I give you some cash, will you buy me something?"

"I'm not sure I should go. Kellan's probably—"

"With the doctor. They just took him for another scan to check the swelling. Probably need to make sure that hard head of his didn't get scrambled too much."

"Oh. Well, in that case..." She turned to Emma. "I'm ready when you are."

"Awesome!" The quirky woman did a little fist pump. To Asher, she said, "Will you let Trace know where we'll be? And text me what you want. In fact, see if the other guys want something, too. I'll put it on the office credit card."

"Sweet." Asher gave Emma a high five. "You're the best, Em."

"I know." She teased. "Why do you think your team leader is marrying me?"

"Touché," Asher hollered over his shoulder as he walked away.

Hooking Mia's arm with hers, Emma said, "I'll tell you the story of how Trace and I met."

"That interesting, huh?"

There was a sparkle in her hazel eyes when she looked over at Mia and grinned. "Let's just say I, too, have some experience with explosions. Come on. I'll give you all the crazy details over coffee."

Minutes later, Mia was staring over at Emma with a coffee in hand and her jaw on the floor. "The entire office blew up?"

"The whole thing." Emma took a sip of her iced coffee. "One minute I was talking with Jake, R.I.S.C.'s owner, and the next... Kaboom!"

Emma's story about a revenge plot against the entire R.I.S.C. organization, explosions, and kidnappings sounded like something she'd see on the big screen. Unfortunately for the other woman and Trace, the experience had been very real.

"You guys are lucky no one was seriously hurt."

"Or killed." Emma nodded. "I mean, Jake and Mac were knocked out pretty good. Mac woke up not long after, but Jake was in a coma for a few days. It was touch and go for a while, but the guy's as tough as they come."

"Who's Mac?"

"She's one of Alpha Team's two snipers."

"She?"

"Yep." Emma arched a thin brow. "But don't let the gender fool ya. That woman can kick ass with the best of them. Including Charlie Team."

"That's cool that they allow a woman to be a part of a covert security team like that."

"Let her, hell." Emma snorted. "She's the best sniper they have. Of course, she's also married to Sean. He's the other sniper on the team, and my brother."

"Wow. Sounds like the teams are more like family than co-workers."

"We are. And since you're with Kellan, that makes you part of the R.I.S.C. family, too."

"Oh, I'm not...I mean, I don't..." Mia blew out a loud breath. "I'm not sure what we are, yet."

With a teasing tone, Emma said, "Yeah, well, you've kind of had a lot going on."

"You can say that again."

The two women were quiet for a beat while they savored their drinks and became lost in their own thoughts. It wasn't long, however, before Emma began asking more questions.

"What are you hoping for after all this is over?"

Mia set her cup down and studied the woman sitting across from her. "Is that your way of asking what my intentions are with Kellan?"

"Pretty much."

They both chuckled, and she waited for it to die down before answering.

"Kellan and I haven't really had the chance to talk about the future."

"But you do want a future with him? Right?"

Mia smiled. "Yeah. I'd like one. Of course, there's the small matter of my husband."

"Meh." Emma waved that away as if it were no big deal. "That'll all work itself out. What's important is you love Kellan, and he loves you."

The comment left Mia blinking. "How did you...I mean, we haven't even said—"

"Remember when you said Charlie team is like a family?"

"Yeah..."

"Well, families talk. And men are even worse at gossiping than women."

"The team's been talking about me and Kellan?"

"Oh, yeah." She shot her an incredulous look. "That's how I know Kellan loves you."

"We've known each other a week."

Emma swallowed another sip of her cool beverage and shrugged. "So what? Trace and I met, fell in love, and had made plans to move in together in that same amount of time."

"Really?"

"Were you not listening to my story earlier?"

"I was. It just seems really fast."

"There isn't a hard set time frame for love, Mia. For some, it's like a slow burning fire. It starts with a tiny spark that eventually grows into a roaring flame. For others, it's instant. A lightning bolt that strikes when you least expect it. That's how it was with me and Trace." She smiled wistfully. "And from the sound of things, that's how it's been with you and Kellan."

"I guess." Mia nodded. "Except, I have no idea if he feels the same way about me."

"Only one way to find out."

"You think I should ask him."

"Of course, I do. Just...put yourself out there and see what happens."

"I started to." Mia admitted softly. "But then the nurse came in, and I—"

"Escaped to the bathroom?"

"Yeah." She chuckled. "And look how that turned out."

"Hey, now. I think it turned out pretty well. After all, if you hadn't gone in there, you would've missed your chance to tell Snatchy McSnatcherson off."

The other woman's pet name for Elliot's mother had Mia coming close to spitting out the drink she'd just taken.

"This is nice." She wiped some coffee that had dripped down her chin.

"Spitting coffee out your nose is nice?"

Mia laughed again. "I meant, spending time with a friend. I pretty much lost all of mine after I married Elliot. It would be nice to have one again."

Reaching across the table, Emma put her hand over Mia's and said, "Like I said. You're part of the Charlie Team family, now. Although, I feel I should warn you. Those guys are seriously overprotective. Like…big brothers who are trained to kill."

"I've noticed." Mia smiled.

"Here are the to-go drinks you ordered." One of the baristas brought over a disposable drink tray filled with four large, steaming cups.

"Great. Thank you." Emma gave the woman a toothy grin as she took the heavy tray from her hand. "Guess we should get these to the guys while they're still hot."

"You carry those, I'll get ours."

"Thanks."

Mia had just started to stand when a man she hadn't seen in three years approached their table.

"Hello, Mia." Elliot's father offered her a nod. "I was wondering if I could have a word with you…in private."

What was this, the family reunion from hell?

"I already spoke to your wife, Stuart." Mia reached for

Emma's cup. "I don't really think there's anything else for me to say."

"But there are things *I* need to say." His aging eyes implored her. "I know my family has treated you poorly, but I really think you'll want to hear what I have to say. Please." He paused. "It's about Elliot."

"Mia, you don't have to—"

"No, I'm okay." She glanced over at her new friend. "If he knows something that can help us find Elliot, I need to hear it."

"Are you sure? Because I can totally stay."

"It's fine, Emma. Really. I've got this."

Still not one hundred percent convinced, Emma told her, "I'll take these to the guys, but then I'm coming straight back." To Stuart, a man she didn't know, Emma warned, "FYI, there are five well-trained men just down that hallway who will kill anyone who even thinks about harming this sweet woman."

With a final parting smile, the tiny spitfire grabbed her coffee and carefully pushed it down between the other four before giving her a wink and walking away.

Oh, yeah. We're going to be very good friends.

More than ready to get this next awkward conversation over with, Mia motioned to the chair across from her and said, "Okay, Stuart. You heard the lady. You have about five minutes to say whatever it is you came to say."

After that, she was going back to Kellan's room. Because there was another conversation that needed to be had. One she'd started with him earlier.

And suddenly, as she sat across from the man who sired the Devil, himself, Mia found herself more than a little excited to finish it.

13

"I still can't believe you let her talk you into such an asinine plan," Kellan grumbled. "You could've gotten her killed."

"First of all, the plan wasn't *our* idea. It was Mia's." Rhys came to his team's defense.

"And second?"

Rhys stared back at him. "The plan wasn't asinine. It was actually pretty smart."

"And brave."

The men in the room all turned to see Emma walking into the room. She spoke as she passed out coffee to everyone but him, since he was still waiting on the Doc's okay to have something more than the disgusting black coffee his nurse brought him earlier.

"Thanks, baby." Trace gave her a quick peck on the lips.

"You're welcome." She smiled up at him before giving Kellan the stink-eye. "I'm sorry if it seems like I'm overstepping, but instead of being mad about what Mia and these guys tried to do, think about how hard it must've been for her."

Kellan jerked back. "You think I haven't?"

"I don't know." Emma's shoulders fell with a loud exhale. "All I *do* know is that woman of yours risked everything to try to end this nightmare for you both. She was willing to face her own personal monster in order to help capture him. It didn't work, but it still took a lot of guts for her to try. Trust me." She gave him a sad smile. "I know a little something about facing your demons head-on."

Wrapping an arm around his fiancée's shoulder, Trace kissed Emma on the top of the head.

Kellan had heard the story of the hell Emma had gone through. But she'd been lucky. She'd found a way to escape her kidnappers and save herself...but not before she was forced to kill two of them.

Watching Emma and Trace now, Kellan realized he not only wanted what they have. He needed it.

A week ago, he'd tried convincing himself they were an anomaly. That true love always ended badly.

But after spending the last few days with Mia, Kellan knew those earlier feelings were wrong. They'd stemmed from having a shitty childhood with a shitty dad. A man Kellan was terrified of becoming.

Thanks to Mia, he now understood that he was nothing like his father.

He wasn't perfect by any means. But he was a good man. A caring man. And he loved that crazy, brave woman with all his heart.

"She's right, McBride," Rhys's deep voice pulled him away from his thoughts.

"You're defending her, now?" Kellan's brows shot up. "Surprising, since you haven't bothered hiding your distrust for the woman.

"I can admit when I'm wrong." Rhys met his stare.

"Look, I know I haven't been as supportive of her as I probably should have, and I may have let some personal shit cloud my judgement, but Mia was ready to take one for the team because she couldn't stand the thought of something else happening to you. Putting herself at risk like that for you...I don't know. I guess it changed the way I look at her."

"Maddox is right." Greyson threw his two-cents in. "Seems to me, you should hang on to this one."

Wearing a goofy as fuck grin, Asher nodded in agreement. "Mia's got my vote, too. But just so you know, I already put my name in the hat in case you decide you don't want her."

To this, Kellan responded with, "You even think about it, I'll rip your fucking heart out and shove it down your goddamn throat."

The room erupted with chuckles as Greyson's phone began to ring. Glancing at the screen, he mumbled something about taking the call outside as he walked into the hallway.

"Guess we know where you stand as far as Mia's concerned." Emma stared up at Kellan with a wide smile.

"Speaking of which, where is she?" Kellan glanced at the door. "I thought you two went together to get the coffee."

"We did," Emma confirmed. "Her father-in-law showed up right as we were about to head back here. She asked me to give them a minute to talk, so I told her I'd bring these to you guys, and then go rescue her from what looked to be a very uncomfortable situation."

Kellan's pulse spiked and his spine stiffened. "What the hell is Stuart Devereaux doing here?"

"Probably came to get Shane," Trace guessed. "Didn't you say he was being discharged today?"

Shit, that's right. "I almost forgot. We were coming here to see him when the bomb went off."

"Dude, maybe you should lie back down," Asher suggested.

Maybe he's right.

"You get back in bed, and I'll go get Mia," Emma offered. "If you're lucky, maybe she'll offer to kiss your boo-boo."

Kellan and the others watched as the woman who kept their professional lives in order waggled her brows and walked away.

"Damn, Winters." He smirked. "That's quite a woman you have there."

Trace beamed with affection when he smiled. "Don't I know it."

As he stood with his team, Kellan thought about what they'd all said about Mia and her willingness to use herself as bait.

It was an incredibly dangerous thing to do. Stupid, even. But damn if a part of him—a big part—wasn't proud as hell.

You should tell her that.

He needed to tell her everything. How proud he was of her. How he'd fallen head over ass for her. All of it.

Turning to get back into bed, he'd just made a silent vow to do just that as soon as she got back when Greyson returned from taking his phone call in the hallway.

"That was Lucas Hall." To Kellan, he explained, "Luke's a former SEAL who's now a detective with Richmond's Major Crimes unit. He and his team were with us at the meeting that never happened."

"He find something?" Kellan asked.

"Unfortunately, no." Greyson's long hair moved across his shoulders when he shook his head. "According to Luke, Devereaux's in the wind."

"There's no sign of him anywhere?"

"Nothing. RPD's had boots on the ground since we left to come back here, but there's been no sign of him anywhere."

Fucking great. "So we're back to square one." Kellan ran a hand over his jaw.

Greyson shook his head again. "Not necessarily."

"What do you mean?" Rhys spoke up again.

"I mean, sometimes the lack of evidence is evidence in and of itself."

"Without the riddles, please?" Rhys drawled.

"There hasn't been any activity on Elliot Devereaux's accounts since two days ago. No credit card purchases, nothing with his bank account…"

"I don't understand." Asher frowned. "How exactly does that help us?"

"The lack of electronic trail tells us that he has to be using cash or someone else's cards. If it's cash, that shit will eventually run out, which means he'll be looking for a handout from someone else."

"His parents," Trace got on board with Greyson's train of thought.

Greyson gave their team leader a tip of his chin. "Most likely. I'll keep an eye on Stuart and Catherine Devereaux's account activity, as well as the brother's. It might take some time, but if they're helping him financially, we'll know it."

"Sounds good." Trace nodded. "In the meantime, I think we should get out of here and let Kellan get some re—"

"She's gone!" Emma rushed back into the room.

Her face was flushed, and her eyes looked precariously close to filling with tears.

"What are you talking about?" Trace went to her. "Who's gone?"

"Mia!" Regret poured off her as she turned her watery

gaze to Kellan's. "I'm so sorry. I thought she'd be safe there. I mean, there were people everywhere, and I thought—"

"It's okay, baby." Trace pulled her close. "It's not your fault."

"Are you sure she didn't just go to the bathroom again?" Asher asked.

"I checked." Emma wiped away a fallen tear. "She wasn't there. There's no sign of her or Mr. Devereaux."

"I need clothes." Kellan's tone was deadly. "Now!"

"Emma, honey." Trace looked down at his fiancée. "Will you go see if you can hunt down a pair of scrubs in Kellan's size?"

"I'll be as fast as I can."

Emma raced out of the room as Trace turned to Greyson. "Pull up hospital security. Check the cameras at the coffee shop, hallways, elevators and stairwells...all of it."

"He has her." Kellan could barely breathe for the fear. "That son of a bitch has her."

"We don't know that for sure," Asher tried—and failed —to ease his worry.

"*I* know." Kellan stared back at his well-meaning teammate. "Mia wouldn't have gone anywhere with her father-in-law. And sure as hell wouldn't have just taken off to go somewhere else without checking in with one of us, first."

Elliot got to her. Right down the hall from his fucking room. And the bastard had used his own father to do it.

"Here!" Emma returned as promised. "These should fit."

Grabbing the set of clothes from her hands, Kellan muttered a warning for her to turn around so he could change without flashing her. Yanking the I.V. catheter from his hand, he ignored the dripping blood, barley waiting for Emma to turn her head before he stripped off his gown and threw on the thin pants and top.

Pulling the drawstring tight, he slid his feet into his boots, which he'd found in one of the cabinets earlier, and started for the hall.

"Where are you going?" Emma asked.

"To find Mia."

Minutes later, after scouring the entire floor, Kellan felt as though he was being eaten alive with terror.

"They couldn't have gotten far," Rhys commented. To Greyson, he asked, "How's the search coming?"

"Finally got in. This place has surprisingly good security." The brilliant man stood with his tablet in his hands and everyone hovering around him. "There." He tapped the screen to enhance the image. "That's when she was still with Emma at the coffee shop."

"Fast forward to where the father-in-law shows up," Kellan commanded.

As asked, Greyson sped the recording forward until they saw the other man approaching the women's table. Kellan watched as Emma walked away and Mia sat back down.

The video had no sound, but he could tell she wasn't happy to be talking with the Devereaux patriarch. Even so, their conversation continued for a few more minutes before they both stood up to leave.

Looking around them for any sign of a possible threat, Kellan held his breath as he waited to see what had happened to the woman who'd snuck her way into his heart. As the recording continued, his greatest fear unfolded before his very eyes.

Kellan and the others watched in horror as Stuart Devereaux pulled Mia in for a hug. She slapped at her neck, almost as if she'd been stung by a bee, and almost immediately began to sway.

Seconds later, her limp body fell into the other man's arms.

Ah, god.

"Rewind that," Trace ordered. "Go slower this time and zoom in on her neck."

The group watched it again in slow motion. When Greyson zoomed in like Trace had instructed, they could barely make out the syringe in Stuart Devereaux's hand.

"Motherfucker!" Kellan hissed. "The son of a bitch drugged her."

Nausea churned in his gut to the point he felt physically ill.

"Wait, who's that?"

Forcing himself to keep the contents of his stomach down, Kellan and the others continued watching the small screen as another man approached Mia and the man holding her.

Wearing scrubs and pushing a wheelchair, Kellan initially thought the guy was a member of the hospital staff. That maybe he'd seen her pass out and had taken her to be checked out.

Maybe that's it! Maybe she's down in the E.R.!

But after the man in scrubs placed Mia into the chair and spun it around toward the elevators, the camera caught a clear image of his face. Greyson froze the screen so they could get a good, hard look.

"Holy shit!" Asher exclaimed. "That's Elliot Devereaux. Are you telling me, that bastard was here the whole time?"

"That's not Elliot." Kellan studied the image closely.

Confused, Asher turned in his direction. "What are you talking about? We've all memorized this guy's face, so we'd know who we're after."

"In all the pictures you studied, did you ever see a scar like that on Elliot's forehead?" Kellan challenged.

Asher looked back down at the screen again. "No." He shook his head. "I don't remember him having a scar like that."

"Because he doesn't." Kellan swallowed. "But Shane Devereaux does."

14

Mia woke with a throbbing headache and a mouth that felt like she'd been chewing on cotton.

At first, she struggled to remember *why* she felt so bad. Had she partied too hard last night?

No, that couldn't be right. She didn't party. Not anymore.

Then why do I feel like I drank an entire bottle of cheap wine?

Laying down on her back, she turned her head and noticed a tender pull in the left side of her neck. It wasn't until she tried to rub the sore area that she realized she couldn't.

Blinking the sleep from her eyes, she glanced down and saw that her wrists had been bound together with plastic ties.

Oh, god!

An instant and fierce panic set in, and she immediately began trying to pull her hands free. The unforgiving plastic dug into her skin, but she kept on in hopes that the blood would somehow make it easier to get loose.

Looking around, Mia discovered she was in a dark,

damp basement. The walls were made of stone, and the place reeked of stale dirt and mildew.

Knowing Elliot had to be the one behind her abduction, her mind raced to remember how he'd gotten her here, and where she could be.

Think, Mia. You have to calm down and try to remember.

Pushing herself into a sitting position, she closed her eyes and did her best to focus through the hazy fog. It slowly started to come back, but only in small, fractured pieces.

Like a puzzle, Mia worked to fit the pieces together in order to make the complete picture.

Coffee. She'd been drinking coffee. Emma was there, and they were at a hospital. Why were they at the hospital?

She was going to see Shane. He'd been shot, and she'd wanted to see him before he was discharged. But she wasn't going there alone.

Kellan.

Her heart kicked against her ribs as she remembered the explosion. Kellan had been hurt in the blast.

She could see him now. Lying unconscious on the ground.

An ambulance had come to take him to the hospital. They'd let Mia ride with since she had no way to drive herself.

The team was there. Emma was there. Mia remembered going to the bathroom and an argument with Elliot's mom.

His dad was there, too. Remember Elliot's dad.

And just like that, all the pieces fell into place. She'd been drinking coffee with Emma when Stuart Deveraux had suddenly appeared. He'd wanted to talk. Apologize for his wife and son.

He'd fallen over himself trying to make her understand why they'd treated her the way they had. Mia distinctly remembered being surprised at the way Stuart had put all the blame for Elliot's abusive behavior onto Catherine's shoulders.

It was her fault, he'd said. Stuart had also told her Elliot had inherited his abusive personality from his mother.

The nervous man had gone on to tell her a tiny piece of their screwed-up history, and how he too, had fallen victim to spousal abuse. Mia remembered the shock she felt from the man's claim.

According to Stuart, Catherine had been verbally and physically abusing him for years. The longer Mia sat there, listening to everything the man had to say, the more she found herself believing him.

When the conversation came to an end, Stuart had asked if he could give her a hug. She'd obliged, and that's when it happened.

The man who should've been a father figure to her had shoved a needle into the side of her neck and injected something to render her unconscious.

Now she was here, in this musty basement with her wrists tied together and no one around to help.

Kellan's handsome face flashed before her, and Mia's crumbled.

He had to know she was gone. Was probably going *crazy* trying to find her.

You can't wait for someone else to come along and save you. You have to try to save yourself.

Pushing herself up awkwardly, she stumbled her way to a dark metal door at the far corner of the room. Mia tried the knob, but it was locked. Not that she'd expected any different.

Light filtered in through a single window positioned high on the opposite wall. The small, narrow rectangle was one of those traditional basement windows. Even if she could find a way up there, Mia knew she'd never fit.

There's no way out.

Tears of defeat burned the corners of her eyes. She was stuck down here until either someone came for her or she died. Or worse.

Sadly, the thought of dying was more appealing than having to face Elliot again.

No! You will not go down that road again. You're stronger than this. You're stronger than him!

Her subconscious was right. Hadn't she told Kellan earlier she was done being afraid? Wasn't it her idea to be bait for the psychotic son of a bitch?

Those weren't the actions of a coward. They were the actions of a *fighter*. And right now, in this moment, Mia knew to her bones she was in the fight of her life.

The only question was would she win, or would she lose?

A sound came from the other side of the door. A rush of fear spiked through her veins.

Okay, fine. So she was still afraid. But that didn't mean she had to give up.

Rather than let the terror eat her away until she was nothing more than a sniveling fool, Mia chose to use it as the driving force to survive.

Sliding to the side, she'd positioned herself so she'd be behind the door when it opened. She held her breath and waited, watching as the knob began to turn.

The door opened. He stepped inside. And when Elliot was within her grasp, Mia attacked him from behind.

Releasing an animalistic howl, she jumped onto his back and wrapped her bound arms around the front of his neck. Using all her strength, she pulled her arms as tightly as they would go in hopes of choking the asshole until he passed out.

But he didn't fight back. Instead, his touch was almost gentle as she heard, "Mia, stop! It's me! It's Shane!"

Shane?

Why was he here? Had he found out what his family had done? Had he come to rescue her?

Make sure it's really him.

"How do I know it's you?"

"Look at my head, honey." He turned it to the left as much as her grip would allow.

Positioned high on his back, Mia tilted her own head to the side, and there it was. The scar.

"Shane?" Her relief was overwhelming. "Oh, my god! What are you doing here?"

"I came to get you the hell out of here. Now, can you please loosen your hold so I can get you down and cut those damn ties off of you?"

Knowing Shane would never hurt her, Mia lifted her arms up over his head. Gently guiding her down his body, her brother-in-law turned to face her, his expression one that was hard to decipher.

"Do you have a knife?" she asked, then shook her head. "You know what? Never mind. I can run with my hands tied. Let's just go before they come back."

She started for the door, but stopped abruptly when Shane slid over to block her path.

"What are you doing?" She asked, confused as to why he was in her way. "Seriously, Shane. This is no time to play around. We have to get the hell out of here now, before your dad or Elliot finds you here."

"My dad?" He chuckled. "My father is as pathetic as you are."

Mia gasped, her mouth dropping open from the shock of his words. "What? Shane, what are you—"

"God, you really are stupid." Disappointment filled his cold gaze. "I mean, there's dumb...and then there's you."

A sick feeling began to settle deep inside her gut. "You've never spoken to me like that before. Why are you—"

"Oh, I have." His lips curled into a slow, evil smile. "On many, *many* occasions."

With a shake of his head, Mia didn't see his hand flying toward her face until it was too late.

Shane backhanded her so hard, she flew off her feet and onto her back. Her head smacked the basement's hard floor with a thud.

Pain exploded in her right cheek and eye, but Mia fought past it to try to make sense of what had just happened.

"My mother was right," he snarled. "I mean, you can't even tell the difference between your husband and your brother-in-law? Jesus Christ, Mia. How fucking dumb do you have to be?"

Through a set of watery eyes, Mia studied the man closely. His condescending tone sounded just like Elliot's. The way he was looking down at her with disgust and, and his awful, hateful words were an exact match to the way her husband had treated her before she'd ran away.

But it couldn't be him. The man standing over her wasn't Elliot. It was Shane.

Sweet, caring, inappropriately funny Shane. The man who'd helped her escape his own brother's torturous hell.

"The scar," she whispered. Mia was staring right at it. "Elliot isn't the one with the scar."

He grinned. "Honestly, I've been wearing it for so long, I forgot it was even there.

Wearing it?

"Shane, what are you—"

Mia watched in horror as he reached up and began *peeling* the scar away.

Only, it wasn't a scar at all. It was some sort of fake skin. Cosmetic latex that had been made to *look* like Shane's scar.

"No," she breathed.

Her mind raced through every recent conversation she'd had with her brother-in-law.

"That's right, wifey." Elliot—*not* Shane—tossed the rubbery material onto the ground beside her. "Surprise!"

From the corner of her eye, Mia noticed a small circle of blood seeping through the fabric covering Elliot's upper left arm. It was the exact location where 'Shane' had been shot.

"That was you?" She couldn't seem to wrap her mind around what her eyes were seeing. "I don't understand. Shane came to my apartment. He said he was trying to help me..."

"That was *me*." Elliot rolled his eyes. "Try to keep up, would you?"

"Where is he?"

"Oh, that's a funny story, actually. Shane *did* call and tell me he knew where you were. Said that if we met on that gravel road, he'd give me all the information I needed to be able to find you."

"So the story about the two of you meeting near the cemetery was—"

"True. I just switched somethings around a bit to fit my agenda."

"You're not making any sense." Her aching head swirled with confusion and disbelief.

"Aren't I?" Elliot released a frustrated huff of a breath. "Fine. I'll dumb it down for you. When you left

Denning that night, you humiliated me. I gave you everything you could ever want. *Everything!*" he screamed that last word. "And you left me as if I was nothing to you."

"I left because you beat me and then put a gun to my fucking head."

"I couldn't let you get away with that kind of behavior." He continued speaking as if she hadn't said a word.

Some things never change.

"It's been two years, Elliot." Mia winced as she pushed herself into a seated position.

"And I've been looking for you ever since! I called in favors... Hell, I even hired the best P.I. money could buy. For two fucking years, there was nothing. It was like you vanished into thin air. Until a couple of weeks ago, that is."

Mia wracked her brain to try to figure out what could've happened to lead him to her, but there wasn't anything that came to mind.

"I see those pathetic little wheels of yours turning, so let me save us both some time. You had a client reach out to you wanting a book cover designed. An author by the name of J. L. DeVoe. That ringing any bells?"

"I remember the job, but that still doesn't explain how you found me."

"Actually, it does. You see, an ad popped up on my social media account. Of course, I recognized your work right away. I contacted Mr. DeVoe. Said I was an aspiring novelist and wondered if he'd be so kind as to share the name and contact information for his cover artist. Which he gladly did." Elliot chuckled. "I still remember the moment I saw his email. Clever move, using your grandmother's maiden name."

"So it *was* you." Mia thought back to the recent times

she'd felt eyes on her. "You were watching me. Following me."

"Guilty as charged."

"Why? If you knew where I was, why go through the trouble of playing all these games?"

"I knew you'd never come back to me willingly," he said as a matter of fact. "But Shane, well, he was a different story, wasn't he? You and he always had a special bond. I accused him of sleeping with you, which of course, he denied."

"We didn't." Mia shook her head. "It was never like that with us."

"But you felt safe when he was around, didn't you, Mia?"

"Yes."

"There's your answer." He drew in a breath and exhaled. "I thought if you were scared, you'd go to him for help. So I came up with the idea to become him. That way, when you turned to him for comfort and advice, you'd really be coming to *me*. It was quite a brilliant plan, don't you think?"

"All except for the part where I didn't go to Shane for help." *You arrogant ass.*

"No." All signs of humor left Elliot's face. "You didn't. You told me, well *Shane,* to go back home so you could play house with that fucking security guard!" He leaned down and grabbed a fistful of her hair. Mia cried out from the fiery pain but refused to let any more tears fall. "It was supposed to be me!" Spittle flew from his lips as he yelled. "Instead, you went to *him*."

"Because I thought you were Shane!" Mia yelled back. "I went to Kellan for protection because I didn't want Shane getting hurt!"

Elliot's shoulders shook with the same, condescending chuckle she despised. "Tell me something, *wife*. How did that plan work out for you and my dear brother?"

Mia thought about what he wasn't saying. "Where is Shane?" She demanded. "What did you do to him?"

"My brother refused to tell me where you were." Elliot shoved her head away with a rough push. "So, I shot him."

Her stomach dropped. "You *what?*" She glanced at his arm. "But you're the one who—"

"Oh, this?" Elliot lifted his arm and inspected the covered wound. "I did this to myself. Hurt like a bitch, but you sure came running to that hospital to see me, didn't you? By the way," he grinned. "That look on your face right now? Totally worth the pain."

"Tell me where Shane is!" Mia yelled.

"Right this minute?" Elliot shrugged his good shoulder. "At the bottom of that little lake near the road where we met. At least, I hope he's still there. I made sure he was dead before I loaded his pockets down with rocks and tossed him in the water. Asshole nearly ruined my plan, showing up at your apartment right after I'd trashed the place. I couldn't just make him disappear, too, though. A missing wife *and* a missing brother? That would be awfully suspicious, don't you think?"

Mia physically gagged as the realization that the man that had been her friend and the brother she'd never had, had been killed because he was trying to keep her safe.

Oh, Shane. I'm so sorry.

Blocking out the immense pain and heartache the loss caused, Mia forced herself to stay focused and keep Elliot talking. The longer she kept him talking, the better her chances of being found.

"That's why you told your staff you were on vacation," she surmised. "So you could kill Shane and then become him."

"Ding, ding, ding!" Elliot held his hands out to the side.

"Ladies and gentlemen, we have a winner!"

The man was even more psychotic than she'd originally believed.

Dear God in Heaven.

He was never going to let her go. At best, he'd keep her locked away like some sort of caged animal. At worst, he'd kill her.

Mia's only chance of survival was to run. So that's exactly what she did.

Knowing he wouldn't expect her to fight back—because she never had before—Mia linked her fingers together to make one large fist and swung her arms up toward his face.

Hitting him square across the nose, she nearly smiled when she felt the bones there give way. The sickening crunch turned her stomach, but she didn't stop there.

"You bitch!" Elliot cried out and held both hands to his face to stop the bleeding. "You broke my fucking nose!"

That's not all I'm going to break.

Bringing her right foot back behind her, she swung it up toward his crotch with as much force as she could muster. Elliot cried out again and dropped to his knees.

The sound of gagging reached her ears as she ran past, leaving him on the floor bleeding and writhing in pain.

Running through the door and up a set of concrete steps, Mia found herself in an old farmhouse. Footfalls came from somewhere behind her, and she knew she'd have to act fast if she was going to escape.

Sprinting through the kitchen and living room, she made it to the front door seconds before Elliot got to the top of the stairs.

Fumbling with the knob, she threw that door open and took a precious moment to study her surroundings. There was nothing but trees, a field, and an old decrepit barn.

Knowing the trees were her best option, Mia started down the porch when she heard him stomping through the house behind her.

"Go ahead and run," he taunted. His voice came out nasally from the recent trauma to his nose. "There's no one around for miles. It's why I had Mother buy this place."

Catherine was in on it too?

Jesus, his was one screwed-up family.

Laughing as if he didn't have a care in the world, the arrogant asshole wasn't even running anymore. It was as if he knew she'd never get away, so he wasn't even bothering to make much of an effort to stop her.

But Elliot underestimated her. He always had.

Mia looked at the trees again, realizing they were too far away from where she was. She'd never make it there before he caught up to her. But if she could make him *think* that's where she was going, she might just have a chance to get away.

Heading in that direction, Mia made sure he saw her through the window. The minute he walked out of her view, she made a sharp left turn and ran back around the side of the house.

Like most older farmhouses, this one had a huge wrap-around porch. Thankfully, it also had a section of lattice that had been broken away, and the hole was just big enough for Mia to crawl through.

Dust and dirt filled her nostrils as she half-crawled, half-scooted across the ground on her hands and knees back toward the front of the house. Not an easy task, given her wrists were still bound together.

From above, she could hear Elliot moving around on the porch.

"Where, oh where, could my little Mia have gone?"

The sound of a round being loaded into his pistol's chamber turned the blood in her veins to ice.

He's just trying to scare you. He won't shoot you. He hasn't had his fun with you, yet.

Praying the tiny voice was right, Mia clamped a hand over her mouth to keep from making a sound. She watched and waited, doing her best to ignore the cobwebs and dead insects scattered around her.

"Come out, come out, wherever you are!"

From her low vantage point, Mia could see Elliot's boots and the bottom half of his legs as he walked along the length of the porch. She forced her lungs to draw in small, shallow breaths as she curled herself up tighter and waited.

Elliot walked around the side of the house, out of her line of sight. She paid close attention to his voice as he continued yelling for her, and she could tell when he got farther and farther away.

When she heard him coming around the opposite side, Mia began crawling back toward the hole.

If she could get out while he was still on the other side of the house, she could make a bee line to the trees from there. Once she got into the cover of the woods, her chances of making it out of this alive would greatly improve.

Moving as fast as she could on her hands and knees, her body was half-in, half-out of the hole in the lattice when she heard the voice from her nightmares.

"Told you, I'd find you."

No!

Before Mia had the chance to move, Elliot's boot came flying down toward her face. A flash of pain struck, and then...

Nothing.

15

Eighteen hours. It had been eighteen *fucking* hours, and still there was no sign of Mia.

Kellan had felt pain before. In his home while growing up. On the battlefield next to his fellow Marines.

But none of those experiences held a candle to the soul-wrenching pain he was feeling now.

I can't lose her.

"We're going to find her, Kellan."

He looked up from his seat at Charlie Team's conference room table to find Asher's determined gaze holding strong and steady.

Always the goddamn optimist.

"Really, Asher?" Kellan snapped back. "That's great news, but there's just one problem with that claim. Wanna take a guess at what that might be?"

"Ease up, Kel." Greyson looked at him. "He's just trying to help."

"We all are," Rhys added.

"This is helping?" Kellan chuckled humorlessly. "We're sitting on our asses while she's out there, going through God knows what because that son of a bitch has her!" His booming voice echoed off the shiny new walls.

"We're doing everything we can to find her," Trace reassured him.

"We don't have a single fucking lead, Winters. Not one goddamn clue as to where they took her. Elliot's parents and his brother have all gone missing, and the security footage and CCTV cameras only show them as far as the interstate. After that, we got nothing!"

Kellan shot up from his chair so fast, the damn thing toppled over behind him. Unable to continue listening to a bunch of bullshit lines that were getting them nowhere, he stormed out of the room without so much as a single word to anyone.

With his nerves shot and his heart shattered, he headed down the main hallway toward the office's reception area. He had no idea where he was going, and at this point, he didn't care. All he knew was that he couldn't spend another *second* in that chair just sitting...and waiting.

He had to do something. He needed to find something that would tell him where she was. And Kellan had been doing this kind of thing long enough to know, he wasn't going to find what he needed sitting on his ass in a fucking conference room.

For the last eighteen hours, his only purpose for living had been to find the woman he loved. And he'd failed.

They all had, but it would be Mia who paid the price.

She could already be dead.

No! He couldn't think like that. He couldn't even entertain the *idea* that she wasn't still alive. Once he started down that path, there'd be no turning back.

"McBride," Trace hollered for him from behind.

Kellan stopped just shy of opening their office door to

face him. "What?"

"Where are you going?"

"Just need to get some air."

With a worried nod, Trace said, "Don't go too far. Just in case."

Meaning, just in case they got that big break in the case. *Right.* Because the universe loved him that much.

Kellan pulled the door open and left. At the end of the larger hallway separating their office with two others across from them, Kellan slapped the button on the elevator. When it didn't come fast enough, he changed his mind last-minute and took the stairs.

Running down the four floors to the ground level helped rid him of some of his pent-up energy, but it wasn't enough. Shoving the metal bar with more force than necessary, Kellan opened the door at the bottom of the stairwell and charged into the building's large, open entrance.

He ignored the startled looks he was getting from people as he marched past. Pushing open one of the two main glass doors, he stepped out onto the sidewalk and turned right.

Kellan had no idea where he was going, and he didn't care. At least if he was walking, that meant he wasn't just waiting around for a string of good luck to come their way.

The others may believe in that shit, but luck had never really been his thing. Kellan wasn't charmed, and he never had been.

From the day he was born, he'd been dealt a shitty hand. The military had been a way for him to escape. To become someone other than the kid whose shithead dad murdered his mom.

For a while there, Kellan had thought he had a good life. He'd been a decorated Marine. He'd been offered a coveted spot within the R.I.S.C. organization.

Then one day not long ago, a petite blonde with mesmerizing eyes and a smile that reached his soul ran her car into the back of his. From that moment on, things began to change for him.

He didn't understand it at first. Had refused to recognize it for what it was. But then he'd heard her laughter as they'd fallen together on the ice, and that was it. That was the moment he knew.

I can't imagine a world without her in it.

Mia Devereaux hadn't just worked her way into his heart. She'd stolen the whole damn thing. And as Kellan walked aimlessly down the busy sidewalk, he came to a very real, and very dark conclusion.

If they couldn't find Mia before it was too late, he may as well die right along with her.

His phone dinged with an incoming message, forcing him away from the macabre thought. Praying it was good news, he pulled it out and tapped the screen, his hope waning when he saw it was just a text from Greyson asking him if he was okay.

Squeezing the phone to the point his knuckles turned white, Kellan barely resisted the urge to chuck the fucking thing into the street. No, he wasn't okay. He'd never be okay again.

Not until I find her.

Without bothering to respond, he shoved the phone back into his jeans' pocket. A few steps later, the guilt began to sit in.

Damn it, he knew his teammates were trying to help. *Everyone* seemed to be trying to find Mia. His team. Richmond P.D. All of them.

But unless some big break just happened to fall into their lap...

"Mr. McBride!"

Kellan's steps faltered when he heard someone calling his name. Glancing behind him, he could hardly believe who it was.

"Mr. McBride, wait up!" Stuart Devereaux jogged down the sidewalk to catch up to him. The silver-haired man was huffing and puffing like he smoked twelve packs a day. "I need to talk to you."

A crimson red haze filled Kellan's vision. He didn't think about his next move. He simply acted.

Filling his fists with the front of the man's jacket, he swung Mia's father-in-law around and threw him against the side of the building.

The man grunted and winced as the back of his head hit the hard brick wall. Kellan didn't care.

"Where's Mia?" he growled, the words escaping through a set of clenched teeth. "I know you took her, so don't bother fucking lying. Tell me where she is right this fucking second, or I swear to God—"

"That's why I'm here!" Stuart yelled. "I-I came to tell you where she is."

"Bullshit." Kellan didn't believe him. "You expect me to believe you just up and had a change of heart?"

"Yes!" The other man's head nodded up and down frantically.

"Why?"

"Because I...I've done a lot of bad things in my life, but that..." Stuart's brown eyes became watery from unshed tears. "I-I haven't been able to sleep or eat. I feel so bad about—"

"You feel *bad*?" Kellen drew his fist back and slammed it against the man's jaw. Fresh blood oozed from Stuart's nose and mouth. With his face right next to Stuart's, his voice lowered to a lethal tone as he warned, "That was child's play compared to what I'm going to do to you if you're lying to me."

"I'm not." Devereaux huffed. "I swear. I don't care what happens to me. I just want this whole thing to be over."

Kellan's gut reaction was that the man was telling the truth. Stuart Devereaux looked tired and defeated. His brown eyes dull with acceptance and regret.

"Where is she?" he asked again.

"M-my left jacket pocket. I wrote the address down so I wouldn't forget."

Keeping his grip steady with one hand, Kellan used his other to reach into the man's pocket. He pulled out a scrap of white paper and unfolded it.

Written on it was an address. A *Richmond* address.

She's still here!

He held the paper close to Stuart's face. "You're telling me this is where Mia is *right* now?"

"Yes."

"Why should I believe a fucking word that comes out of your mouth?"

"Because it's true!" Actual tears left silver streaks down the man's aging face. "I swear I'm not lying."

"Why come to me now? You could've left town and gotten away with this whole thing."

"I can't take it anymore." Stuart's bottom lip quivered with his trembling chin, and his voice thickened with regret and shame. "The lying. The pain. My wife, she controls it all. She always has. Then, as Elliot got older, it was the two of them against everyone else. Shane was..." The man's face started to crumble, but he regained his composure and finished what he was saying. "Shane was the only good thing in my life, and Elliot..." His breath hitched. "Elliot took him from me."

"Shane's dead?"

Stuart nodded. "Elliot killed him. H-he...he concocted this crazy plan to pretend to be Shane so he could get close to Mia again."

Pretend to be...

Kellan didn't understand what the man was going on about, and he didn't have time to care. The only thing mattered was Mia, and this man was the key to finding her.

"Come on." Kellan pulled Stuart away from the wall and shoved him back in the direction from which he came.

"W-where are we going?"

"To my office."

"What are you going to do to me?" A flash of fear crossed the man's eyes.

Not what I'd like to, that's for damn sure.

"First, you're going to tell me and my team everything you know about that address and what your son is planning to do."

"And then?"

Kellan opened the door to his building, his cold gaze landing on Stuarts as the man walked past. "Then I'm going to find your son, and I'm going to kill him."

Several minutes later, Kellan and the rest of Charlie Team had the full, fucked-up story. Once Stuart started talking, he couldn't seem to stop.

He told them all about how Elliot's finding Mia was a fluke. Something about a design of hers he'd come across, and how he'd used that to track her down.

Stuart sat in his chair, his thin body trembling with fear.

He told them when Elliot had first come to the city he'd decided to play around with Mia before finally making his move.

The stalking. The brake lines. Her apartment. It was all Elliot. Stuart even shared that Shane Devereaux knew Elliot had found Mia, so he'd come to town to warn Mia.

Stuart even gave them all the details about how Elliot had killed his own brother and took his place in hopes of tricking Mia into turning to him for comfort and safety. He also told them that Catherine Devereaux had purchased the property where Stuart claimed Elliot was holding her for the sole purpose of keeping her held captive there until she learned her lesson.

It was at that point when Kellan leapt across the table.

Lucky for Stuart, Kellan's teammates intervened to keep him from ripping the guy's head off right then and there.

The whole sordid story sounded too unbelievable to be true. Except, Kellan believed every twisted word the man had shared.

Sometimes the truth really is stranger than fiction.

His team, however, wasn't so quick to jump on board.

"This could be a trap," Rhys commented when the room had settled back down. "How do we know they didn't plant another fucking bomb at this farmhouse of theirs, and they're just waiting for us to show up so they can take us all out?"

"I'm telling you the truth." Stuart uttered sternly.

Asher snorted, "Yeah, because you've proven to be such an upstanding guy before now."

"I understand your hesitation in believing me, but I can prove to you that I'm telling you the truth. Here." He pulled his phone from his jacket pocket. Pulling up a picture, he turned the screen toward Kellan.

"See?"

Kellan looked closely, his blood boiling with rage when he realized the man was right.

In the picture, he could see Shane Devereaux carrying Mia inside. Walking beside him was Catherine Devereaux.

Fucking bitch.

"You took this?" Kellan glanced up at the man.

"As I was leaving, yes." Stuart nodded.

Made sense, given that the photo appeared to have been taken from the inside of a car.

"Why?" He needed to know.

"I wanted proof. Something I could use against them later."

"Later." Kellan clenched his jaw. "So you were planning to just *leave* her there?"

"I didn't have a choice! My wife and son...they would've killed me, too, if I'd tried to stop them."

"There's always a choice, Mr. Devereaux." Trace glared at the other man.

"You took that picture in case you got caught." Greyson chimed in. "You wanted something to use as a bargaining chip in case the D.A. offered you a deal."

Stuart nodded shamefully.

"And you're *sure* Mia is still there?" Kellan asked. Because right now, that was all he needed to know.

"Yes." Stuart turned to him. "But you need to go to her now. You have to stop him, before it's too late."

"Too late?" Trace watched the man closely.

"I talked to Catherine this morning." Stuart swallowed hard. "She's back home, in Denning, pretending as if nothing ever happened." He grimaced. "She told me Elliot's planning to change locations first thing tomorrow."

"He's taking Mia somewhere else?" Trace asked. "Why?"

"According to Catherine, Elliot doesn't feel safe being this close to you and your team. When he first picked the property, he wasn't expecting..."

"What?" Kellan prompted him.

Stuart's empty eyes rose to his as he simply stated, "You."

A stretch of silence passed before Rhys spoke up again. "What do you think?" He looked around the room. "Do we trust him?"

With nausea churning through his stomach and fear clawing its way through his heart, Kellan stared back at his friend and said, "We don't have choice."

"He's right." Trace nodded from the front of the room. "Gear up, boys. We'll leave as soon as Detective Hall gets here to take this asshole away."

Because Greyson had called his friend the minute Stuart Devereaux had begun talking.

According to Greyson, Hall wanted *his* team to be the ones to check out the address Stuart had given them while Charlie Team escorted Stuart to the precinct. But Kellan had shot that idea down fast.

This was Mia they were talking about. Sweet, loving Mia.

And there was no one else on the planet Kellan trusted more to get her out of that hellhole alive than his own team.

Eight minutes later, Detective Lucas Hall entered the conference room and placed Stuart Devereaux under arrest. Those eight minutes waiting for Greyson's former SEAL buddy to arrive were the longest of Kellan's life.

Or so he thought.

But as they drove to the address Stuart had given them, he realized he'd been wrong. According to their company SUV's GPS, the farmhouse where Mia was being held was twenty minutes away.

Charlie Team made it there in ten.

16

"They're going to find you," Mia rasped. Her throat was beyond dry from lack of water. Her empty stomach had stopped growling hours before.

I'm teaching you a lesson.

That's what Elliot had said when she woke back up with her wrists tied to a pipe in the basement ceiling. He'd said it again when he'd beaten her black and blue, refusing to give her food or water.

He was trying to break her. Make her never want to leave him again. Over and over during his abusive rants, he'd tried making Mia believe her place was at home with him.

I'd rather die.

A hysterical laugh escaped her dry throat as she hung there, the tips of her shoes barely touching the basement floor. If someone didn't find her soon, that was exactly what was going to happen.

She was going to die in this basement. Broken and alone. And the only thought on her mind was…

Kellan.

God, she was going to miss him. Her biggest regret in life

—marrying Elliot, included—was that she never told him how she felt.

Now she was going to die, and he would never know.

The muscles in Mia's arms and shoulders burned as they were stretched to the point of nearly tearing. Her eyes stung with the need to cry, but her body was so depleted of water, even her tears refused to fall. It was for the best, really

Crying took energy, and right now, she needed to save every single ounce she had left.

A noise reached her from above, pulling her away from her inevitable train of thought. She listened closely as the movement sounded again, and she realized someone was walking around upstairs.

The movement started out softly, at first, but soon grew in intensity and speed.

What's he doing?

The stomping became more erratic. It grew closer and closer, until the basement door flew open, and Elliot ran purposely toward her with a knife.

"No!" Mia tried to scream, but it came out as more of a crackling rasp. Ignoring the pain it caused, she began pulling against the rope in an effort to get free.

It was useless. The rope didn't budge. And Elliot... Elliot was standing in front of her, now. His blue stare cold and hard as he raised the knife toward her.

"P-please," Mia begged. "Elliot, don't—"

He reached up and cut her wrists free.

Mia cried out as a thousand sharp needles cut through the skin on her arms all at once, the blood flow they'd been denied rushing through her depleted veins.

"Come on." Elliot wrapped his meaty hand around her upper arm and began dragging her behind him.

"Wait!" She tried to fight against his strong hold. "Where are we going?"

"We're leaving."

Exhausted and weak, Mia's sluggish form struggled to keep up. "W-why are we leaving?"

"Your boyfriend found us."

Kellan?

"He's here?" Mia gasped. A renewed sense of hope left her pulling against him with more strength than before.

Elliot swung back around, his face red with anger. But there was something else there.

Though his fight against it was valiant, she could make out the fear hiding behind his dark gaze.

"Yes, he's here. The security system I set up when Mother bought the place alerted me to activity on the north side of the trees. Your precious *Kellan* is here, along with those teammates of his. And unless you want to see them all die, you'll hurry the hell up!"

Shoving her up the stairs, Mia stumbled twice, before a rush of renewed strength spread through her. If Kellan was here, that meant she had a chance.

A chance at living...and love.

When they got to the top of the stairs, Elliot grabbed her by the arm again. He yanked her forward so hard this time, she thought he'd rip her already tender shoulder right out of its socket.

Mia fought him off as hard as she could. She kicked and screamed, clawing away at him with her flailing free hand.

"Fucking stop!" Elliot swung the hand with the knife around, the wooden hilt smacking her in the side of the head.

"Ah!" Mia cried out, the fight in her momentarily

stunned as she struggled against the white dots flashing before her eyes.

"Try that again, and next time I'll use the blade."

Filling his fist with her hair, Elliot forced her to start moving again. They made it two stumbling steps before Kellan and his team burst through the front door.

Their guns were held out in front of them, their taut arms holding the weapons steady. All five men had their eyes locked on Elliot, and their barrels were aimed directly at Elliot's head.

Mia's knees nearly gave out with relief.

"Let her go!" Kellan yelled. The look on his face telling.

Though Kellan would never risk hitting her, Mia knew the first chance her sweet, deadly man got, he would pull that trigger and end this nightmare...without ever looking back.

But Elliot still had the knife in his hand, and the chickenshit bastard had just put her body in front of his to use as a human shield.

Putting the blade to her throat, her husband said, "Drop your guns, or I'll slice her ear to ear."

Focused solely on Elliot, Kellan's voice sounded lethal as he warned, "Put the knife down and let Mia go, or I swear to God, I will shoot your ass where you stand."

In pure Elliot arrogance, he refused to admit he'd lost.

"Are you deaf, or just stupid?" he spat out the words. "What, you don't think I'll do it?" His voice became erratic. "I'll kill her right *fucking* now!"

Mia winced as the tip of the blade pierced the skin at her neck. Kellan's gaze turned to stone as his finger slid down and curled around his trigger.

This was her warrior. Her hero. *He* was the man she loved.

A man standing before her now, willing to kill to protect her.

Mia didn't want it to come to that. She didn't want Kellan to have that kind of dark mark on his soul. Not because of her.

"Please, Elliot," she rasped. "Listen to him. There's still a way out of this, if you'll just—"

"Shut up!"

That blade pricked her skin again.

"You have two seconds to drop it, or I drop you," Kellan promised. "Your choice."

"Fuck you!" Elliot shouted.

"One..."

"You won't shoot me. Not while I have this knife to her—"

"Two."

A loud blast filled the entire house. Something warm and wet splattered the side of Mia's face. There was a sharp flash of pain at the side of her neck, and then...

She was falling.

"Mia!"

She landed on top of Elliot, her back to his front. Kellan ran to her. He flung Elliot's limp arm—and the knife that had fallen onto her chest—away from her.

Dropping to his knees, he was surprisingly gentle as he pulled her to her feet and into his arms.

"Oh, thank god!" Kellan breathed. "I'm so sorry. So fucking sorry."

"I'm okay," she cried. "I'm okay."

Mia wasn't sure who she was trying to convince more... him or herself.

But Elliot was dead, and Kellan was here, so yeah. She was going to be okay.

"I'm so fucking sorry we didn't get here sooner." Kellan pulled back just enough to look her in the eye. When he took in her bruises and swollen eye and lip, the rage she'd seen before returned ten-fold.

"His death was too easy," he rumbled. "I should've made him suffer."

"He's suffering now." Of that, she had no doubt.

"What about you?" He looked her over with an assessing glance.

Mia knew he was asking about her physical state. If she was hurting which, yeah...she was. But her bruises and sore muscles would heal. All that seemed to matter now was...

"I'm free."

Tears filled Kellan's eyes as they flew back up to hers. With a softened expression, he gently cupped her face and pressed his lips to hers. "Yeah, sweetheart. You are."

HOURS LATER, AFTER STATEMENTS HAD BEEN TAKEN AND THE doctors had poked and prodded her, Mia lay in her hospital bed with Kellan by her side.

"I can't believe it's really over."

"Believe it." He lovingly brushed some hair from her forehead and tucked it behind her ear.

She was covered in bruises and every inch of her body was sore. But she was alive, and Kellan was with her. Everything else would sort itself out later.

"What's going to happen to Elliot's parents?"

"They've been charged as accessories in your assault and kidnapping, as well as being accessories in Shane Devereaux's murder." Kellan lifted the hand that didn't have the I.V. attached to it and brought it to his lips. "Greyson's detective friend said he spoke with the D.A. She assured him the judge will deny bail, which means your in-laws are both behind bars, where they'll stay for the rest of their miserable lives."

Tears fell from Mia's eyes. Not because she felt sorry for Stuart or Catherine. Not even a little bit.

No, her heart broke for what Elliot had done to Shane. His was a loss she'd feel forever, and it would be a long time before she stopped feeling guilty for his murder.

She stared back at Kellan, so very grateful she'd rammed her way into his life.

They still needed to finish the conversation she'd started back when he was in the hospital. Mia was going to wait until later to bring it up, but the realization of how short— and unpredictable—life really was had her opening her mouth and letting it all out.

"I love you," she blurted. "You can tell me I'm crazy or that you're nowhere near there yet. It's fast, I know, so really, it's okay. Because no matter what your feelings are for me, it doesn't change the way I feel about you. And after everything that happened, I just thought..." Mia swallowed against the knot of emotion suddenly filling her throat. "I just wanted you to know."

For the longest time, Kellan didn't say a single word. He just sat there, holding her hand while his gray eyes stared back into hers.

When Mia was certain he was going to say something totally lame like 'thank you', Kellen leaned up and pressed his lips to hers in the softest, most loving way.

Then he whispered, "I love you, too."

Her heart kicked against her ribs, but she had to be sure. "You don't have to say it just because I did."

"I'm not feeding you some bullshit line, Mia." His lips curved upward. "I thought I was crazy for thinking I could fall in love with someone so quickly. But then you were taken from me, and I knew…"

"Knew what?"

"That I didn't want to live without you." He kissed her again, careful of her healing lip. "I love you, Mia Devereaux. My heart and soul…they're yours for as long as you want them."

"Forever," Mia whispered without thinking. She held her breath and waited for his response.

Putting her mind—and heart—at ease, Kellan smiled wide and said, "Forever sounds like a perfect start to me."

Mia leaned up and kissed *him* that time, her heart so full she thought it would burst.

This is what true love looked like. What it *felt* like.

Love wasn't about pain and fear. It also wasn't intimidation and arrogance.

No, true love was kind and sweet. Supportive and passionate. And Kellan McBride, well… He was all those things and more.

And the very best part of it all?

He. Was. Hers.

Asher Cross walked across the hospital parking lot. Pulling the collar of his jacket up to protect his neck from the wintery breeze, he made his way through the row of parked cars to his own.

He still couldn't believe how lucky they'd gotten. If Mia's father-in-law hadn't decided to give himself up, she would either be out of the state or dead.

Either scenario would've left Kellan broken beyond repair.

As he pushed the button on his fob, Asher began picking up his pace. This case had left him tired and emotionally drained. And Mia wasn't even his to fear losing.

She belonged to Kellan. His teammate and friend. As far as he and everyone else on Charlie Team was concerned, that made her one of them. So yeah, he'd been worried. For her and for Kellan.

Thankfully, it all worked out in the end. Now they could start building their new life together, and Asher couldn't be happier for them both.

A little jealous, maybe.

Driving home, his heart felt a bit heavy as he thought about the empty house waiting for him. The feeling took him off guard, because he was only twenty-nine, after all. It wasn't like he was ready to settle down or anything.

But after months of Trace and Emma walking around the office talking about plans for their wedding, and now seeing the way Kellan and Mia were together... Asher found himself thinking more and more about the prospect of finding that one person to spend the rest of his life with.

Someone to be there when he got home from an op. A woman who would love him with all her heart, the same way his mom had loved his dad.

They'd been partners in every sense of the word. Right up until his mom had taken her last breath.

That's what Asher wanted for himself. Someday.

A woman's image flashed in his mind's eye as he pulled into his driveway and put his car in park. A beautiful doctor with long brown hair and eyes the color of dark chocolate.

Ever since his team had rescued Dr. Sydnee Blake from that shithole building in Abu Dhabi, Asher couldn't seem to get her out of his head. He'd even thought about asking Greyson to work his magic and find out her address so he could go to her. Just to check on her and make sure she was doing okay.

But every time he started to ask G to do it, Asher chickened out. He didn't want to come off as some sort of crazy stalker, and if he showed up on her doorstep uninvited, that's exactly what she'd think of him.

He was certain of it.

Yes, he needed to forget all about Sydnee Blake, as well as the prospect of falling in love. His mom had always told him it would happen when it was supposed to...and when he'd least expect it.

Just like it did for Trace and Emma, and Kellan and Mia.

Decision made, Asher pulled his keys from the ignition and got out of his car. Suddenly tired to his bones, he trudged up the sidewalk to what had once been his childhood home. Planning to take a long, hot shower to wash away the last few days before bed, he put the key into his lock and turned it.

Asher was reaching for the doorknob when a set of headlights lit up the front of his house. He turned, expecting it to be Greyson or Rhys, but the car wasn't one he recognized.

With the lights blinding his view, Asher couldn't make out the person approaching him until she was standing only a few feet away from him.

Long, dark hair. Eyes he'd been dreaming about since he last saw them. A body with curves he'd give his right hand to touch.

It's her.

Blinking quickly, Asher was almost certain his eyes were playing tricks on him. Until he heard her voice.

"Hi, Asher." Dr. Sydnee Blake stared up at him with a nervous smile.

"Sydnee?"

"I-I'm sorry to just show up like this," she spoke in a rush. "I know it's highly inappropriate, but I...I didn't know where else to go."

Finally getting over the shock of seeing her again—and that she was actually here, at his home—Asher noticed for the first time how nervous she appeared to be.

No, not nervous. Scared.

Dr. Sydnee Blake from Washington D.C. was at his house, and she looked fucking terrified.

Asher's spine stiffened, and he took a step toward her. "What's wrong?"

"I need your help."

"Okay." He didn't hesitate. "With what?"

With a nervous lick across a set of full, kissable lips, the gorgeous woman stared up at him and said, "I think someone's trying to kill me."

Want to see how Asher and Sydnee get their Happy Ever After?

Pre-order Asher (Charlie Team 2), releasing April 2022!

ALSO BY ANNA BLAKELY

Charlie Team Series
Kellan
Asher
Greyson
Rhys

R.I.S.C. Series

Taking a Risk, Part One
Taking a Risk, Part Two
Beautiful Risk
Intentional Risk
Unpredictable Risk
Ultimate Risk
Targeted Risk
Savage Risk
Undeniable Risk
His Greatest Risk

Bravo Team Series

Also by Anna Blakely

Rescuing Gracelynn
Rescuing Katherine
Rescuing Gabriella
Rescuing Ellena
Rescuing Jenna

Marked Series
Marked For Death
Marked for Revenge
Marked for Deception
Marked for Obsession

TAC-OPS Series
Garrett's Destiny
Ethan's Destiny (March 2022)
Beckett's Desire (July 2022)
Slade's Future (November 2022)

WANT TO CONNECT WITH ANNA?

Newsletter signup (with FREE Bravo Team prequel novella!)
BookHip.com/ZLMKFT
Join Anna's Reader Group:
www.facebook.com/groups/blakelysbunch/
BookBub: https://www.bookbub.com/authors/anna-blakely
Amazon: amazon.com/author/annablakely
Author Page:
https://www.facebook.com/annablakelyromance
Instagram: https://instagram.com/annablakely
Twitter: @ablakelyauthor
Goodreads: https://www.goodreads.com/author/show/18650841.Anna_Blakely

Printed in Great Britain
by Amazon